THE LIBRARY

FROM

OF

Federico

HELEN GRIFFITHS

Federico

ILLUSTRATED BY SHIRLEY HUGHES

HUTCHINSON JUNIOR BOOKS

HUTCHINSON JUNIOR BOOKS LTD
3 Fitzroy Square, London W1

London Melbourne Sydney Auckland
Wellington Johannesburg Cape Town
and agencies throughout the world

First published 1971

This book has been set in Joanna type, printed in Great Britain
on antique wove paper by Anchor Press, and
bound by Wm. Brendon, both of Tiptree, Essex

ISBN 0 09 107110 0

Contents

Storks over the village

Antonio Torres came out of the classroom, hopped down six of the stone steps which led to the playground, and jumped the last four. The books under his arm scattered all over the asphalt, but he didn't care. He was first out of the classroom because he was the only boy to get all his sums right and he felt very pleased with himself.

He picked up the books, replaced the middle pages which had fallen out of one of them, then sat on the bottom step. There wasn't much point in being let out first, because he couldn't go home without his younger brothers, but at least his father would be pleased when he heard about the sums.

Antonio was small for his nine years, a bit on the thin side, and the white smock that was obligatory school wear accentuated the darkness of his eyes and close-cropped hair. While he sat on the step with the books beside him, he remembered the bubble-gum screwed inside a piece of paper in the smock and fished it out.

He couldn't get all the paper off, but once it was all chewed up together, it didn't make any difference to the flavour. He still didn't know how to make proper bubbles, they always plopped into holes, but it was as good a way as any to pass the time.

The school playground was in the shadow of the church. In the summertime this had its advantages, but now, in February, it was very cold and Antonio shivered as he scraped the bubble-gum off his lips with his teeth and tried yet again to make a real bubble.

He looked up at the sky, which was already gloomy with encroaching dusk. His view was broken by the tall church tower and it was here that he fixed his gaze. He wasn't really looking at the tower itself but upon the mass of old black twigs, so much a part of the building itself that no one ever noticed them.

The first storks had built a nest there a hundred and thirty years earlier, when the tower had been completed, and from then on there had always been a pair of storks in the village, probably descendants of the original pair. At the end of summer the storks went away. To Africa, Antonio's father said, or to the southernmost parts of Spain. They didn't come back until the beginning of spring.

'How do they know when it's springtime?' Antonio had wanted to know.

'I'm not sure. Perhaps it's a feeling they have inside. Perhaps it's something in the air. They always live on the highest roof-tops so they can feel the changes in the air better than we can, sitting by fires and wrapped up in jerseys.'

Antonio watched for the storks every day. The teacher had said that the first official day of spring began on March the 21st, but he knew that the storks would be back before then. They didn't go by calendars. They came when they felt spring in the air.

It was the same with the donkey. All through the winter she had been growing fatter and more slothful.

'In the springtime she'll have a baby donkey,' Antonio's father, Señor Torres, had said.

'But when? When?' they had all wanted to know, equally anxious to see and touch the promised arrival.

'I don't know the exact date,' he had protested with a laugh. 'But it'll be in the springtime, right at the very beginning.'

Then Antonio, who was the eldest, had wanted to know how they could tell when the spring would arrive.

'Watch out for the storks. When you see them spring-cleaning the nest on the church tower you can be sure that spring's arrived. It always seems that everything starts to happen once they get here.'

'And will the baby donkey come then?' Marieta wanted to know. She was just five, the youngest of the family, and the only girl.

'Probably. We'll have to let you ride him.'

Antonio said, 'I'd like to look after him. I've never seen a baby donkey.'

'Me, neither,' whined Miguel. 'Papa, if Antonio can look after him, so can I. It's not fair that he . . .'

'And what about me?' broke in Juan. He was six and didn't like to get left out of anything.

'And me?' said seven-year-old Alberto stolidly.

'At first the foal will be looked after by its own mother. She'll be able to manage quite well on her own. Donkeys make very good mothers. After that . . .'

He paused, and five pairs of eyes, equally dark and round and big, were fixed upon him. Whatever he said was final.

'After that we'll put Antonio in charge of him because he's the eldest.'

There were groans, and cries of complaint from the

three younger boys. Only Marieta clapped her hands and said, 'Yes, yes. Antonio must look after him.'

Antonio had smiled to himself, feeling very important. It wasn't every boy in the village who had a donkey of his very own to look after.

It was just as the other boys came pouring down the steps, jumping, hopping, sliding, shouting, pushing and joggling with their arms and legs, that Antonio saw the storks. They suddenly appeared in the sky, two dark shadows against the fading sunlight. He had taken them for pigeons, but, as they drew closer, steadfast and unerring in their flight, he saw they were far too big for that.

'Look!' he cried. 'Look!'

The tone in his voice, the eagerness with which he pointed, attracted even the attention of the most unruly. The shouting and tomfoolery stopped as most faces turned skywards.

'The storks!' cried Antonio.

Two black and white birds, male and female, flapped gracefully down to the tower. They shook their wings and strutted about, showing no sign of having travelled perhaps hundreds of miles.

The boys in the playground watched and then they began to shout a greeting to them, jumping up and down, glad of any excuse to make a noise. Satchels flew in the air and soon the teacher was coming down the steps to find out what all the excitement was about. But none of them knew about the baby donkey because still it hadn't been born.

*

Antonio lived in a typical Mediterranean cottage in a small village on the island of Mallorca. The house was built of local sandstone and its owner had never bothered about having its walls plastered and whitewashed, which would have made it more attractive. Nor had he bothered about having glass panes put in the window-frames. This didn't matter in the summertime, but in winter the house was either cold and damp or airless.

Over the years a number of natural adornments had lessened the plainness of the bluff little house. Red and white geraniums grew in a wilderness about its walls, often reaching higher than the kitchen window until they were hacked down again. A grape-vine had crept up past the door to the bedroom windows and its leaves and branches were a jungle of pathways for the cats and pigeons.

There were only four rooms in the little house, apart from the larder under the steep staircase which was almost a room in itself, and three windows. The windows all looked on to the piece of land that was included in the rent; a long narrow orchard with almond and plum trees, orange, lemon and pomegranate.

Most of the produce of the orchard belonged to Antonio's father and he had to work very hard to make the earth yield all of which it was capable. He grew broad beans and melons, artichokes, cabbages, potatoes, onions and garlic, each in its proper season. Then there were tomatoes and red peppers which Antonio's mother threaded on to long strings and hung up on the walls of the barn to dry.

Señor Torres needed the donkey to help him with the

ploughing, to carry his saleable produce to the market and to fetch the straw he needed for the pigs. He could just about afford to keep a donkey and she had been occupying the orchard for as long as Antonio could remember. During the daytime she rarely had anything to do, unless it was Sunday or a holiday, because Señor Torres worked all day long away from home.

He could do all sorts of things, but wasn't skilled enough in one particular trade to have a steady income. Sometimes he would be in the mountains, cutting down trees; sometimes he was working at the construction of one of the many new hotels being built beside the sea; and once he worked in an hotel, looking after the boilers and the swimming pool.

There were nine people altogether in Antonio's family, his brothers and sister, his parents and his maternal grandparents. When his parents had first come to Mallorca from the south of Spain, before he was born, his grandparents had lived in the little house too. They had all come together, looking for work because in their own village there had been none. The natives of the island didn't like the people from the mainland. They called them 'foreigners' just as if they were German or French or English, and although Antonio's family had lived in the same house for ten years and had even learned to speak the island dialect, they were still called 'foreigners' by their neighbours.

As the family grew larger, the house seemed to get smaller and so the grandparents went to live in a two-roomed cottage half a mile away. Antonio knew very little about the owner of the house in which he had been born. He came once a month to collect the rent and complain because the children had broken something or because he had seen them swinging in the trees.

His father called him Mestre Pedro and said he was both a misery and a miser. He had a large farmhouse out in the country with plenty of good land which produced fruit and vegetables of every kind, and yet he was so mean that rather than give away the overripe fruit that fell from the trees, he would bury it in the ground.

Because he was the eldest, Antonio was expected to look after the rest of the family. He had to get them all to school on time and bring them safely home again. If seven-year-old Alberto broke the neighbour's window Antonio got the blame for not keeping his brother out of trouble. If eight-year-old Miguel lost his sweater on the way home from school Antonio was slapped for not noticing. If Juan pulled Marieta's hair then he was expected to smack his brother and stop his sister's wails.

There were some advantages in being the eldest, like having pocket money and being allowed to go to the pictures on Sunday afternoon, or going on the bus to Palma with his grandparents, but the disadvantages weighed far more heavily.

When he gave orders to his brothers they didn't always obey him. They answered him back when he scolded them, but he wasn't allowed to defend himself when his parents blamed him for one of their misdeeds. The fault was always his responsibility. It was very unfair because, although he was allowed to hit his brothers, his hand didn't hurt half so much as his mother's, which he felt more than anyone else.

Their mother, María, was harassed by housework and the care of all the animals. She was always cooking and cleaning, ironing and sewing, washing and scrubbing, determined that her home should be as bright and as clean as that of anyone else, in spite of its humble appearance and numerous occupants.

She didn't have time to spend affection on her children and was often in a bad mood. When she did feel like fussing one of them it was Marieta who got most of the attention because she was the only girl. Then Juan, who was only a year older and often hung about her, then Alberto and Miguel, who did nothing but fight all day long but managed to make everyone like them.

Antonio was silent and withdrawn, watching over his brothers and sister with almost paternal zeal but receiving little in return. There were moments of pride, when his father singled him out for something special, or when the bit of extra money that came unexpectedly into the house was spent on a new pair of trousers or shoes for him. But these things didn't make up for the feeling of loneliness that was often with him.

His brothers rarely wanted to play with him. Marieta was the one who loved him most, but her idea of sharing his company was making him help with her numerous dolls, and he escaped that as often as he could.

Therefore he was especially pleased when his father said, 'Antonio must look after the baby donkey,' because at long last he would have something that would be his alone, something that would love him for all the care he was determined to bestow, and he watched his father's donkey every day, wondering if she would ever produce her tardy offspring.

Didn't she know that the storks had arrived and were already nesting in the tower? Didn't she know how much he intended to love her foal? It was to be the most exciting event of all his nine years, but the imperturbable donkey neither knew nor cared.

Donkeys in the orchard

The chocolate-brown donkey belonging to Antonio's father was in the orchard, knee-deep in the new year's barley, a bit muddy, a bit scruffy, round as a barrel and looking about to burst. The barley was grown especially for her. There was hardly any grass in that part of the world and for three months of the year the orchard was turned over to barley for her. She ate it while it was still green, then she ate the sun-bleached stalks, and after that she had to wait another nine months before there would be such a luscious item in her diet again.

It was very peaceful in the green, tree-shaded orchard. The only sounds were the grunts of the pig in the nearby sty and the faint throaty calls of the pigeons. Normally the donkey would have been happy on her own, with no one to trouble her and all that delicious barley on every side, but on that sunny February afternoon she was far from contented and even her appetite had deserted her.

She hunched up beside the thick black trunk of the oldest almond tree, her favourite, and from which she had often nibbled bits of bark in the past, sighing from time to time and restlessly shaking her head. Dusk stole over the trees and barley tops but no one came to see her.

It was not until Señor Torres returned from work and took the usual bucket of swill to the pig that anyone came near her. Even then he didn't look at her closely. He just noticed her darker bulk against the darkness of the twilight as he tended the excited pig, and tutted impatiently because Antonio had forgotten to take her in.

16

'Antonio!' he yelled and, when the boy appeared, 'Come and fetch the donkey.'

He watched the thin, shadowy figure approach, saw him halt abrubtly and then heard him cry, 'Papa! Come here! Be quick!'

'What's the matter?'

'It's the baby donkey. He's here. In the grass. Do come.'

Antonio knelt in the dew-damp barley, shivering in the evening chill, shivering with excitement. Even he could see that the foal was only about five minutes old. It must have been born just before his father went out to feed the pig and was lying unseen in the deep grass, not yet able to use its legs.

'Oh, Papa, isn't he beautiful!' he exclaimed as his father came and stood beside him. 'You said he'd be born when the storks came and you were right.'

The mother donkey had drawn back a little in Antonio's presence, but now she had grown in confidence and forgotten about him, returning to her task of nuzzling the foal all over and licking warmth into him.

'We'd better get him into the stable. It's getting cold. I'll carry the foal. You go ahead and spread some straw on the floor for him.'

The stable was in the part of the house beneath Antonio's bedroom and next door to the kitchen. There was a door from the kitchen which led into it, just as if it were another room in the house. In a way it was. It was a place where the children played when the weather was bad, where their mother hung the clothes to dry on a wet day, where things could be stored in case they might be useful again one day, although they seldom were.

On the obscure and dusty shelves about the walls were a conglomeration of tools, straw hats and baskets. There was a stack of tall canes for beating down the almonds at harvest time, a pile of sacks, another of fire-wood and a broken-seated chair which had been put aside for mending and which now sheltered several spiders. In the middle of the stable was the donkey cart and in the farthest corner a wooden partition, behind which was a stone manger and drinking bowl. It was here that the donkey was usually tied up at night.

Antonio was clumsy in his excitement. He knocked over the pitchfork, he dropped half the straw before reaching the stall and he fell over the sack of bran he hadn't noticed. But when at last the two animals were safely in the stable, his father having gently lain the foal in the straw, he had stopped shivering. Now he could feel his face burning with emotion.

The baby donkey began to waggle his ears and blink his eyes and stir his legs. He was all thick beige fur and eyelashes and tiny rubbery hooves that looked far too soft and small for him to stand on.

'Oh, he's beautiful,' Antonio breathed again, hardly daring to speak above a whisper, his eyes shining with wonder.

His father smiled and ruffled his dark head. 'All new-born things are beautiful,' he agreed.

A few seconds later the foal had somehow managed to draw his splayed legs under him and, straightening out the doubles with a terrific jerk, was suddenly almost standing upright. Antonio's exclamation of delight became a gasp of dismay as he just as suddenly collapsed.

He wanted to run forward and pick him up, but his father put a hand on his shoulder and held him back.

'He'll manage,' he said. 'Just watch.'

'What's going on out there?' called his mother from the kitchen. 'What's keeping you both so long?'

'It's the baby donkey. He's arrived!' yelled back Antonio excitedly and in a minute the rest of the family came rushing from the kitchen, pushing and dragging at each other's arms, each in an effort to be first on the scene.

They jogged each other and scuffled in the straw scattered about the floor, all excitedly jabbering at once. The foal pricked his ears and tried to turn his head in the direction of the noise, which was enough to send him tumbling in a heap.

'Supper's ready,' shouted their mother just then, and they all rushed back to the table.

Antonio was the last to leave the barn. Reluctantly he switched off the dim light but left the kitchen door open so that the mother donkey could see her baby and care for him the better. While he ate he could hear the sound of movements in the straw and he didn't even notice what his food was because all he thought about was what was happening in the semi-darkness of the stable.

After supper he went back there. The foal was asleep, curled up like a dog, its muzzle tucked into its flank. The fawn-coloured hair was dry now and stuck out fluffily all over him. Every few minutes the mother donkey lowered her head to sniff at him and rub her muzzle across his back.

When Antonio looked at the foal he felt almost a

pain in his chest. It made him want to cry and jump for joy at the same time. He didn't know why he should feel like this, just looking at that new-born sleeping creature, but he was glad to be alone. At that moment he didn't want to share his feelings with anyone or have them interrupted.

*

In the beginning it was as though the little donkey never stopped growing. When only a few hours old he had been so thin and lanky, his head far too big and heavy for the wisp of body that supported it, and with jerky legs that couldn't possibly bear his weight. But by nightfall of the following day, when he was exactly twenty-four hours old, he was already less out of proportion.

His head was still terribly big and clumsy-looking, but the short little neck was stronger. The large ears, sharply pricked, acted as a balance to keep him from keeling nose first into the straw at every movement. His legs were not now so hopelessly at odds with each other. In a very short time he had learned just what to do with them and almost how to control them.

Antonio could do nothing but look at him. He was deaf to all his mother's commands and to Marieta tugging at his hand, wanting him to come and play. He sat on an upturned bucket, his chin in his hands, looking and looking and all the time finding something new to wonder at.

The way the fluffy hair curled; the softness of the big, innocent eyes; the springy, trembly movements. The more he looked the more he wanted to stay looking, and he was

sure that he had never seen anything so marvellous as this in all his life.

The mother donkey was equally engrossed by her off-spring. She nibbled constantly at different parts of him, as if finding snarls of hair that needed straightening, and wisps of straw stuck to his withers or behind his ears. She was very fussy about keeping him clean and nuzzled him all over a hundred times a day.

The days were sunny and fairly warm and Antonio was told that he could turn both mother and son out to graze. Within a short time the foal could gambol and hop and twist his way from one end of the orchard to the other. He jumped over his shadow, he shied at the orange dandelions, he was frightened of the nervously quick birds, chattering in the trees.

By the time he was a week old no trace remained of the wavering new-born thing Antonio had found in the orchard. He was so confident in everything he did that it was as though he had been a week-old donkey for ever.

Now Antonio was no longer satisfied by just looking at him. He wanted to touch him, crush him in his arms as he had that first night before the foal was even aware of him. He wanted to feel the wondrous thing that his eyes and heart had been following every day.

But the donkey didn't trust him. He was curious about him. He had seen him often enough to accept him as part of the world he knew, just as the trees and the grass and the wind that had always been there. But Antonio was a live thing, with movements as unpremeditated as those of the birds that made him snort and shy, and he was instinctively afraid of anything he couldn't understand.

His reactions were very disappointing and the intense feeling of joy that had overcome Antonio that first night was replaced by a yearning for the foal to care about him too. It was as his father had said. Everything the baby donkey needed was supplied by his own mother. She gave him his food, his warmth, and his love, assuming that a baby donkey needs loving as much as a human baby does, and he had no reason for wanting anything that Antonio could offer.

The only thing Antonio could give him was a name, and he called him Federico.

Rain and its aftermath

In Mallorca most people know what the weather is going to be like at different times of the year. January is a month of sunshine; February is often bitterly cold, with the coldness running on into March. At the end of March the rains usually begin. It rains for hours in drenching downpours, making streams of the lanes, until even the dried-up 'torrents' try to resemble their name by collecting a few pools which trickle into each other.

No one really minds the rain, except that its onslaught is invariably the signal for a cut in electricity, because, apart from the occasional showers in April and May, and the violent summer storms which are absorbed by the heat within an hour, they know there will be no more rain until November or December. The wells under the houses fill up with the water that rushes down the roofs and everyone is careful to catch as much of it as he can.

Antonio liked to hear the rain pouring down the pipe inside the kitchen wall. He could watch it if he wanted to. There was a little wooden door which opened on to the pipe, at the point where it branched in two directions, one to the well, the other out to the yard. When the rain began his mother let it all rush out to the yard for the first quarter of an hour.

'Like that,' she told him, 'all the dirt that's on the roof or in the gutters won't get into the well.'

Alberto and Miguel liked to run out to the yard and hold their hands under the pipe. Water was too scarce to be wasted and this was about the only opportunity they had in the whole year to splash about in it. Antonio had done the same when he was smaller, but now he preferred to lift the heavy iron lid that covered the well in the yard and watch the water rise. He could see his own head, small and shivery on the unquiet surface, moving to the rhythm of the rain music.

When he was in bed Antonio could hear the rain beating on the roof. It crept into the house through the tiles and there was a slow drip, drip, drip on the stone floor. He counted the seconds between one drip and the next. One, two, three, four, drip. One, two, three, four, drip. Each drip came steadily, exactly four seconds after its predecessor, just like a slow-moving clock. He fell asleep to the sound of the steady stream above him and the beat of the leak by the window.

In the middle of the night he woke up. He didn't know what time it was, whether morning was near or still far away. He felt cold. The eiderdown had slipped to the floor. Perhaps it was the cold that had woken him. He rearranged the bedclothes, snuggled under the blanket and closed his eyes. But sleep wouldn't come. Alberto and Miguel were breathing steadily in the bed beside his own and his father was snoring in the next room.

But now the sound of the rain, so friendly and comforting before, troubled him. He didn't know why and tried to ignore the unpleasant feeling encroaching, nightmare-like upon him.

What was wrong? Why did he feel this heaviness, this unease, which the unceasing rain intensified with every passing minute? He shivered, feeling goose pimples all down his back, and then he knew.

That evening some friends of his parents had come unexpectedly from Palma and, what with the surprise, the excitement of unwrapping the presents they had brought, the late supper and one thing and another, he had gone to bed without remembering that the mother donkey was waiting for her supper too and the foal expecting his soft straw bed. They were in the orchard still, the mother donkey tied to the tree to keep her from the onions and cabbages, the foal trying to find warmth and comfort beside her.

Antonio told himself that it wouldn't matter. It wasn't very cold, after all, and the donkeys wouldn't mind getting wet. If they were wild donkeys they would often get wet and have no one to care for them. But, then, wild donkeys were not tied to trees. They could find somewhere to shelter, beneath a rock or among thick bushes. There were caves up in the hills in which to keep dry.

Supposing the baby donkey caught a cold? Supposing he died?

Suddenly the anxiety which Antonio had been trying to keep at bay swept over him. He went to the window overlooking the orchard and, after a struggle, managed to open the shutters. Rain beat in his face and the wind pulled the shutters from his grasp, banging them against the outside walls.

He shivered with cold. He couldn't see the donkeys. There wasn't a star in the sky and the moon was lost behind the clouds. He strained his ears, but the only sound apart from the rain was the wind shaking the trees. What would the donkey and her foal be doing out there in the wet green barley?

The wind caused the shutters to creak and bang and he reached for them in vain. Alberto stirred and began to whimper, and a few seconds later their mother was in the room, hardly recognisable in her long white nightdress and hair curlers.

'What are you doing?' she cried, grabbing hold of Antonio and feeling the wet sleeves of his pyjamas.

'I've left the donkeys out in the orchard. I must go and get them,' he explained anxiously.

'Don't be silly. You're not going out at this hour.'

'But it's so cold and wet.'

'They'll be all right. Besides, it's almost dawn and the rain's nearly stopped. Get into bed now, but take off that pyjama jacket first.'

She pulled a towel out of the chest of drawers and threw it at him, murmuring a few words to Alberto at the same time to stop his sleeply moans.

'Dry yourself with that.'

She pushed him down into the bed and pulled up the eiderdown. Then she reached out into the darkness to find the swinging shutters. As she pulled them to, Antonio thought he could hear a donkey braying. He sat up again, but it was no good arguing with his mother.

'Get into bed,' she snapped at him, raising her hand threateningly, so he dived under the blankets in an instant.

Then she blew out the candle she had brought with her, for there was still no electricity, leaving Antonio sleepless in the darkness.

*

26

When Antonio woke again it was daylight and his brothers' bed was empty. They were all downstairs getting ready for school. He could hear their voices, high-pitched, demanding, and their mother scolding all four of them at the same time. There was the sound of a slap and Juan started to howl.

'Antonio!' She shouted up the stairs, making him jump.

Then he remembered what had happened during the night and rushed into his clothes which were tossed over the iron bed rail. He nearly choked on the glass of milk his mother thrust at him, such was his hurry, and was still tucking his shirt tail into his trousers as he ran down to the orchard to see the donkeys.

It had stopped raining, but the sky was grey and the hill-tops were lost in a cloud of mist. Between the black furrows which his father had ploughed with the mother donkey not very long ago were rivers of water. The barley was half beaten down and the leaves of the almond trees dripped so much that it seemed to be raining still.

The two donkeys stared at Antonio. They looked all right, but he would have taken them to the stable straight away to rub them down with some straw or a dry sack had not his mother shouted after him, 'You're going to be late for school. Leave the animals alone. You haven't time to bother about them now.'

When Antonio returned home at lunchtime he could see that the foal wasn't well. He stood listlessly beside his mother, ears floppy, not even caring when the boy went right up to him and stroked his back. It was the first time he had ever allowed anyone so close. Usually he shied away like a bird when someone approached and no one

but his own mother ever touched him.

The thick woolly hair was soaked right through and the body beneath it was icy. Antonio gazed at the foal, biting his lips with worry. Was it just his imagination or was the little animal thinner than he had been yesterday?

He untied the mother donkey and jerked at the halter. When the foal saw she was moving away he tagged behind her. By his pace, Antonio knew he wasn't well, that he must have caught a chill as he had feared. He was so listless, so slow, and he didn't even lift his head.

As soon as he got them to the stable, Antonio found a sack that wasn't too dirty and began to rub the foal's back and flanks. He rubbed hard and fast, but the mother donkey didn't trust him and tried to push him away with her head. She too knew that her foal was sick.

At first he took no notice of her, but then she began to roll her eyes and lash her tail, lifting a hindfoot with menace. He pulled the halter rope through a ring in the wall and tied her up close, hastily throwing a few handfuls of dry bread into the trough to keep her occupied. But she didn't care about the bread, too anxious about the foal, who was suddenly as thin and forlorn-looking as on the day of his birth, the beige fur rubbed up the wrong way, the legs hardly able to support his weight.

Antonio rubbed with the sack as furiously as he could, growing hot with his efforts but feeling no returning warmth in the little donkey. He didn't know if he was doing any good, but he had to do something. Soon he abandoned the sack, now damp, in favour of a handful of straw, but when he started rubbing the foals' hindquarters the little thing suddenly sat down, almost knocking him over.

There was no way of getting him on all fours again, so Antonio went down on his knees to continue. Perspiration dripped down his face. Soon his shirt was sticking to him and his back ached with the savage will he was putting into the job.

The foal just stretched out in the straw with a sigh, completely still except for the occasional shiver that convulsed his gangling frame, reminding Antonio of the last jerks of a dying chicken. His fingers were so stiff he could hardly move them and he just couldn't rub any more. Desperation and anger seethed in his breast. Everything he did was useless.

Marieta came to see what he was doing. She knelt beside him and put her hand on the donkey's neck.

'Poor thing,' she said. 'Is he very ill?'

'I think so.' His lips trembled.

She watched her brother, impressed by his distress. Antonio didn't often cry, not so much as her other brothers anyway. It seemed to her that he was big and strong, pain-resistant and incapable of hurt. When she saw the tears sliding down his cheeks she grabbed his hand and began to cry too.

'Don't cry, Antonio,' she begged. 'I'll help you get him better. Tell me what to do and I'll help you. But please don't cry.'

Donkeys in the kitchen

It was not until Señor Torres came home from work in the evening that something was done about the foal. Luckily, he came early that night because of the continued bad weather and as soon as he saw Antonio's drawn and anxious face he knew that something was wrong.

Federico really was sick now, his breath coming in deep rasps, his nose and eyes running just as if he had a very bad cold. He didn't even want his milk, although it was long past two of his feeding times.

Antonio watched his father's face while he examined the donkey. He already felt that little bit more hopeful, just having him there, confident that if anything could be done his father could do it. The electricity had returned and in the dim stable light the lined but cheerful features were comforting.

'We must keep him as warm as possible. Tell your mother to build up a big fire in the kitchen.'

It was a wet night again. A blustering wind sent the rain in one direction and then another. It sounded different, according to the way it was being driven. The stable creaked with dampness and a fire would be a good thing. There was a fireplace in the stable itself but it hadn't been used in so many years, and was choked up with so many odd things that it was useless trying to start a blaze there.

Señor Torres had a way of animating everyone with his words and suddenly everyone wanted to help. Juan, Miguel and Alberto filled their arms with twigs and branches that were stored in the stable for just such an occasion as this. Antonio staggered into the kitchen with several thick logs of olive wood, which his mother placed about the flames already soaring through the thin dead branches. His face burned as he watched the dancing, crackling heat and his heart seemed to leap with hope, just like the flames.

Marieta dragged an old blanket to spread over the floor in front of the fireplace. She pushed back the chairs, her cheeks as red as Antonio's from her work in front of the fire, and grew cross when Miguel, Alberto and Juan began tumbling about over the blanket.

'Get off! Get off!' she cried. 'It's for the little donkey. It's not for you. Get off!'

They rolled out of reach of her slaps, laughing at her indignant fury, but quickly scrambled out of the way as their father came in with the donkey in his arms. He wasn't a big man, but he was strong, and he placed the foal carefully on the blanket in front of the high-jumping, erratic blaze.

Normally the cracking sounds as the flames took hold of the twigs would have startled Federico, but now he didn't care where he was or what was done with him.

The mother donkey began braying in the stable, a wild, emphatic protest. Where was her colt? What were they doing to him? At first no one took any notice, but the noise became unbearable.

'Go and untie her, Antonio,' ordered his father. 'Let her come and see what's going on. That might quieten her down.'

'That's it,' scolded María. 'Now we've got one donkey

32

in the kitchen, we might just as well have two.'

It was difficult for her to cook the supper while one donkey took up most of the space on the floor and another poked its head through the door and had to be restrained every few minutes from barging right in. But no one listened to her muttered complaints. They were all fascinated by their father's attempt to revive the foal.

'Antonio, the brandy! Juan, bring some straw! Marieta, get out of the way! Alberto, mind you don't fall into the fire! Antonio, stoke up the logs a bit.'

He lifted the foal's head, forced the top of the brandy bottle between his jaws and tipped it down. Most of the brandy ran out all over him, but some of it must have

gone down the foal's throat to judge by the way he jerked and struggled and coughed.

At his orders, María produced the bottle of camphorated oil which she kept for the children's chests in winter, when most of them started to cough. Antonio poured it into his father's cupped hands and watched him rub it fiercely into the little animal's chest and ribs.

'If we can get him warm, perhaps he'll be all right,' said Señor Torres, and soon he was perspiring as much as had Antonio that afternoon.

The mother donkey had worked her way right into the kitchen by this time and stood beside the man, occasionally pushing at the foal with her muzzle, trying to get him to all fours, reminding him that he must feed. She hawed and squealed and shook her head up and down in distress, while the children covered their ears and cringed, and was very confused by the smell of camphorated oil.

'It's no good,' admitted Señor Torres at last, when he looked at the foal again after supper. 'We'll have to get the vet.'

'That'll cost you some money,' warned María with raised eyebrows.

'And what else can we do?' He sounded angry now. 'We can't let the animal die.'

Antonio transferred his gaze from one to another, torn with anxiety. He knew that money was short. It was one of the reasons why his mother was always cross and hard-working. When she had done all her own work, she worked for other people to earn some money.

When any extra had to be spent there was always an

34

argument between his parents until they decided whether it was worth while or not. Sometimes his father had the last word. Sometimes his mother. He knew she didn't want to spend money on the vet. She didn't even like spending money on medicines for the family if she could find some remedy of her own.

'You've already wasted half a bottle of brandy,' she reminded her husband. 'And most of the camphorated oil. And all those logs which we wouldn't have used except for the donkey.'

'The donkey's worth money. One day we can sell him.'

'If he lives.' There was a pause. Both of them looked at the fire and Antonio held his breath. 'And when you've sold him,' she went on, 'I don't want any more animals about the place. They're more trouble than they're worth.'

By the tone of her voice Antonio could tell she was acceding. He rushed up to her and hugged her tight.

'Thanks, Mama. You're an angel. I promise I'll look after him better next time.'

She pushed Antonio aside and pretended not to care about the hug. But she did care really, he knew she did, only she was so used to being cross that it was no longer easy for her to be nice. She had to be in the right mood and just now she wasn't.

*

As soon as the vet entered the kitchen and saw the foal, he shook his head.

'Not much hope there, I shouldn't think,' he said,

kneeling to run a professional hand over the rapidly wasting frame. 'How old is he?'

'About five weeks,' said Señor Torres. From the expression on his face it looked to Antonio as though he was already regretting having called the vet.

The man shook his head again. 'Donkeys are funny things. They've no resistance. They make up their minds that they're going to die and they just do.'

'Just like that?' put in María, surprised. She couldn't credit a donkey with enough imagination for such behaviour.

'Isn't there anything you can do?' begged Antonio still unable to believe that the little donkey who had been so beautiful and lively only the morning before should now be slipping into almost certain death.

'I could try an injection. But it might be too strong for him. I've only used them on full-grown donkeys and mules before.'

'What else could you do?' asked Señor Torres.

'Nothing really. He's far too small. Just keep him warm and hope for the best. You've already done everything possible.' He glanced at his wrist-watch.

'I'm sorry to have troubled you,' said Señor Torres, noticing the movement. 'It was just that we hoped . . .'

He shrugged, then sighed.

'I'll give him the injection if you like. My bag's in the car.'

'How much is it?' asked María.

'A hundred pesetas.'

She could buy two pairs of shorts for the same amount. Juan and Miguel needed them, but she didn't say so.

'Try it,' said her husband. 'It's better than nothing.'

All the children had experienced various injections and they watched with morbid fascination as he prepared the syringe, the needle—such a big one!—and the alcohol, wondering if it would hurt the baby donkey as much as it always hurt them. Juan rubbed himself, remembering.

But the foal didn't notice. His eyes were shut and somehow he looked smaller and thinner than ever.

'Just keep him warm and hope for the best,' the vet repeated as he put his things away. 'I'll come back tomorrow if he's still alive.'

Antonio went to bed reluctantly that night. Supposing the fire went out and the donkey grew cold on the kitchen floor? Supposing he managed to get up and wandered out to the stable, where his mother anxiously called from time to time? Supposing . . .?

So many thoughts rushed through his head, but the worst of all was thinking of the little donkey dying alone.

In the middle of the night, having lain awake until everyone was asleep, he crept out of bed, pulled his jersey over his pyjamas and went downstairs. He had to cross his parents' room to reach the staircase and held his breath as he tiptoed past the foot of their bed, sure of waking his mother at the slightest untoward sound.

It was so very dark with all the shutters tightly closed, but, fortunately, a faint glow from the kitchen fire reflected on the wall of the staircase, dispelling the utter blackness. The kitchen was warm. He could feel its heat as he came down the cold stone stairs in his bare feet. The fire was low but hadn't gone out. His father had stacked two new olive logs over the embers which would last until morning.

For a moment, Antonio stood on the bottom step, examining the softly lit room with its moving shadows. It looked so different from its daytime aspect that he hardly recognised it as the room in which the family lived and ate and laughed and squabbled. A cockroach ambled across the floor, making his bare toes curl as he saw it, and he was careful where he put his feet as he went up to the foal lying, oh so still, on the rucked and shabby blanket.

He stirred up the red ashes until a flame shot out, flickering light around the walls and catching newly to the half-burned olive log. Then he curled up on the blanket beside the foal and leaned his head against its ribs.

He could hear its heart still beating, thump-thump, thump-thump, thump-thump, and smiled to himself. He stroked his hand all over the stiff beige hide which had lost its softness.

'Don't die, Federico. Please don't die,' he whispered. 'I know it was my fault, but please don't die.'

His face began to burn with the heat from the fire. Warmth stole all over him, dispelling the goose pimples and occasional attacks of shivers. His head felt heavy with sleep and his neck ached. He leaned against the foal, just to rest for a moment. The little animal was feeling warm too. He stroked the sunken flank, remembering a song he had once learned at school and which was often sung at home when Marieta had been small enough to bounce on her father's knees.

'Come on, little donkey,
Let's go to Bethlehem.
Tomorrow is a holiday
And the day after too.'

Come on, little donkey. Come on,' he murmured, and he fell asleep with the words and the tune and the foal's heavy breathing mingling in his ears.

*

Federico recovered. Not all at once, he had been too near to death for that, but as the days went by his strength returned and, with it, his appetite and curiosity. Señor Torres said it was thanks to the injection, the vet said it was just one of those things, but Antonio knew it was because he had spent the whole night helping to keep the donkey warm.

Village events

The time went by and Federico didn't stay small for long. As winter drew nearer and the storks flew away once more, Antonio saw that he was a baby no longer. He didn't even drink his mother's milk any more but pulled up the dandelions that bordered the orchard and ate the tops off the thistles. He was almost as tall as his mother, with long sturdy legs and a chunky body.

Antonio taught him to accept a rope round his neck, a halter round his head, and hobbles round his legs. The donkey fought against everything because he was self-willed and liked being free. But Antonio tried to make the lessons sweet with sugar and other titbits. His patience was endless, the lessons were like a game, and he didn't really mind when Federico was disobedient.

On the 10th of January was the festival of San Anton, the patron saint of all the animals. Federico was nearly a yearling and well trained enough to the halter to be able to take part in the procession which started in the church courtyard and went all round the village. Antonio had never taken part in the event before, and María didn't think much of the idea now. 'I can't see any sense in blessing an animal as pig-headed as that one,' she grumbled, but she ironed Antonio's best clothes especially for the event, wanting him to be as smart as possible.

Antonio's father showed him how to groom Federico until his coat shone. He found an old wire comb and helped him get the dried mud off his belly and fetlocks and, with the kitchen scissors, trimmed his untidy mane and tail. Then he gave Antonio some money to buy coloured paper at the stationer's and, when he returned with the red, green, yellow and blue sheets, showed him how to make rosettes and streamers with which to decorate Federico's halter.

On the morning itself Señor Torres tied red rosettes all the way down the donkey's tail and put another half dozen in his mane. Federico wouldn't keep still, nervous of the sound of rustling paper and not at all keen on so many attentions, and Antonio was very sharp with him because he was as nervous as the donkey and wanted him to look beautiful.

Then it was his turn. His mother combed his unruly black hair with eau-de-cologne in an effort to make the spiky bits stick down. She inspected his hands and knees and rubbed his patent-leather shoes with the duster to bring up the shine, then straightened the little bow tie which was held in place by an elastic band under his shirt collar. She'd bought it only the day before.

At last they were ready to set out for the church. Antonio presented himself in front of the house and all the neighbours came to have a look at him and Federico, as well as all the family. Marieta gave him a kiss.

'You both look ever so beautiful!' she exclaimed, raising a laugh all round, and Antonio blushed.

Juan, Miguel and Alberto stared in awe, hardly recognising the rough little donkey which had inhabited their orchard for almost a year. Federico looked fit for a prince with all his finery. His ears were pricked, his dark eyes brilliant with excitement, his small hooves pranced in the cobbled lane in his eagerness to be off.

He had never been in the village before and Antonio had to hold tight to the halter rope. Every time a motor-bike roared by, which was about every two minutes, Federico nearly went mad.

There were donkey carts on the road ahead of him, covered with arches of green leaves and palm branches, bright with paper streamers and rosettes, just like Federico's. A man went by on a huge black stallion, riding bareback like a Red Indian. Antonio had never seen such a beautiful animal and stood in awe beside Federico to let the snorting, haughty creature pass by, tossing its crimpled mane and flowing tail.

There were the big roan horses that brought the firewood from the hills for the bakery. Today their wagon was loaded with merrymakers who had painted their faces with burnt cork and wore a variety of fancy dresses.

It seemed such a long way to the church, and as he grew nearer, the street became more and more crowded with people. Flags and bunting fluttered in the breeze above their heads and there was so much noise; a record-player blaring out a *paso doble* over a loudspeaker, the clattering of so many hooves, the shrieks of children, the shouts of the young men who pressed their motor-bike horns in a chorus, and the cries of the ice-cream man trying to attract more customers.

Federico shook all over. Antonio had brought a good supply of sugar lumps in his pocket to keep him moving, but when they ran out the donkey just dug in his hooves and refused to budge. No amount of pleading or scolding

42

helped. Some youths tried pushing him from behind, while laughing at Antonio's predicament, but Federico let fly with his hooves until they left him alone.

Miserably Antonio watched everyone pass him by, the dogs with bows in their collars, the mules with jingling bells, the two new-born lambs in the shepherd's arms. Only when the street was quiet and almost deserted would Federico consent to go forward but, by the time they reached the church courtyard, the mass was over.

'Where have you been?' cried Antonio's family, who had gone by a different route, and he could hardly keep the tears from his eyes as he told them.

'Never mind,' consoled his father. 'There's still time to have him blessed. They're queuing up now.'

Antonio took his place in the line, behind a little girl with a fat rabbit in her arms. Federico's ears stood on end as he watched the rabbit and he forgot about his fear. Behind them came an old man with a donkey that looked about as old as his master. Neither were dressed up. Both were very shabby. The donkey began to chew at the red rosettes in Federico's tail.

'Don't do that without permission,' the man admonished, and it looked as though the donkey understood, because he waggled his ears mournfully and left the rosettes alone.

The procession of carts and animals went all round the main streets of the village, to the clash of tambourines from the girls in the wagons, who were also singing folk music at the tops of their voices. They stopped at the tavern for the wine and biscuits which were traditionally offered to them, and they stopped at every succeeding offering of refreshments. It was about the only time of year when the villagers gave anything away. Antonio was enjoying himself now, swallowing glass after glass of thick sweet wine, with hardly time to gobble up the biscuits in between. Federico had most of the biscuits, tugging them out of his fingers and even daring to snatch one from the proferred tray.

It was just as well that Federico knew the way home because Antonio's head was swimming by the time most of the carts and mules and people had dispersed. The donkey's streamers were torn and shabby and the neighbours had forgotten about him. No one was watching their return. Antonio left the donkey to graze beside his mother, who promptly began to pull at what was left of the paper in his tail.

*

Very few exciting things happened in the village. After

44

San Anton there was the annual bicycle race right round the island, when the competitors flashed through the village on their bright metal mounts. Everyone spent half the morning on the cobbled pavements of the main street waiting for them. Then there were ten minutes of excitement while they cheered them on and they were gone for another year.

There were the first communions in April and May, interesting only to the families concerned. But Juan's first communion was not very exciting because it was the fourth in four years and his parents couldn't afford to make a great event of it.

After that nothing special happened at all until the month of August, when the whole village dressed up to celebrate the anniversary of its saint. There were dances in the village on three successive nights and one whole day was declared a public holiday. The streets were decorated with flags and paper streamers, rockets were fired at various intervals, starting at six in the morning, and everyone made as much noise as possible.

That year the mayor decided to try to attract more people to the village celebrations by organising a number of additional events to arouse their interest. He had posters pasted on the walls and stuck in shop windows to advertise the new programme and everyone had something to talk about.

Antonio propped his mother's shopping bag between his dusty, sandalled feet and read the details. Motor-bike races; clay-pigeon shooting; tests of strength and, most exciting of all from his point of view, horse and donkey races.

His imagination was at once captured by the big red letters. Donkey races! Surely his Federico could easily win a race, but when he told his family of his intentions everyone laughed at him.

Antonio felt hot with indignation, and decided that the very next day he would learn to ride his donkey. He didn't think it would be difficult, as long as Federico kept still enough for him to mount. He didn't have a saddle, of course, but all the donkeys in the village were ridden bareback.

There was just a week to the day of the races. Antonio thought he had plenty of time, but Federico had other ideas. He had never done any work in all his eighteen months and, his curiosity forcibly curtailed, had grown to believe that his only duty in life was eating, dozing and biting the mosquitoes off his back.

When Antonio started plomping down on his back and dragging him away from his shady spot beneath the trees he wasn't at all pleased. Mostly he refused to budge. He would shake his ears in irritation, then drop his nose to sniff at the ground and pretend that Antonio wasn't there.

'You'd better use his mother's bridle,' suggested Señor Torres. 'It might be a bit big for him but perhaps we can make it fit.'

The bridle was similar to the halter except that under the noseband there was a ridge of sharp metal which would dig into the tender muzzle every time pressure was put on it by the reins. Federico was so startled the first time Antonio pulled on him, a bit too hard and impatiently perhaps, that he flung up his head, kicked up his heels and threw him to the ground.

Antonio didn't really hurt himself because he hadn't fallen very far, but he was made to realise that he had as much to learn as Federico. He took him to the stony lane that led to the main road, thinking that once out of the orchard the donkey might understand better what was expected of him.

'Come on, Federico,' he said. 'We've got to win one of those races. My mother's always saying you're useless and stupid. We've got to show her she's wrong.'

But Federico just flapped his ears and didn't seem to care. He let Antonio sit on his back and when he felt like walking forward he did so. But each time he scented something tasty he stopped to pull at it, and Antonio could drum with his heels as hard as he liked but he would take no notice. When he felt the sharp metal dig into his muzzle he kicked out swiftly, leaving Antonio rueful and angry on the ground.

One afternoon he tossed him into the prickly-pear tree that grew at the bottom of the lane. The children were always very careful to keep well clear of the stiff jungle of cactus, having learned from sad experience just how treacherous it was. You had only to touch it to find your finger full of the finest, smallest, hair-like thorns. It was far worse than the stinging nettles that grew in its shadow and it sometimes took days to get the thorns out.

Antonio could hardly keep the tears out of his eyes as he picked himself up, collecting more thorns with every movement. He began rubbing his arms and legs with the sand in the lane. There was no other way of getting the thorns out. Federico watched while his young master

47

scrubbed himself frantically, munching at a mouthful of nettles. His dark eyes were white ringed, his ears were still flattened. He looked very cross in spite of the juicy leaves in his mouth.

'I don't love you any more,' Antonio shouted at him, really hating him in that moment. 'You're bad, bad.'

Federico waggled his ears as if to say, Well it was your fault, and in irritation Antonio picked up a stone and threw it at him.

'Take that, and that, and that!' he cried, throwing every stone within his reach, and the frightened donkey careered up the lane as fast as he could go.

'You deserve it,' Antonio shouted after him. 'You don't deserve any kindness at all,' but when Federico had disappeared from view beyond the houses, he began to feel contrite and wished he hadn't lost his temper.

'Federico,' he yelled. 'Come back! Come back!'

He flung down the mixture of sand and stone he was still clutching and stood undecided. He still felt sore all over; there were dozens of prickles itching in his arms and legs. They had even got through his shirt and were itching all over his back, but he was suddenly worried about Federico, dashing off alone and frightened.

Supposing he got on to the road where the big water lorries turned unexpectedly round the blind corner into the village? Supposing one of those tourist cars came along at full speed right into him?

'Federico!' he yelled again, suddenly imagining all sorts of terrible things, and he broke into a run.

Antonio in trouble

The lane which ran from beyond Antonio's house ended
at the main road. There were no houses at this point,
just a few orchards coming down to the road, and, on the
other side, open countryside, wild with gorse and heather
and pine trees. Had Federico taken to the open land,
Antonio would have seen him, for there were no hiding
places. But the white stony slope was deserted except for a
few magpies flitting between the bushes.

So Antonio trotted, panting now, into the village.
Federico was still nowhere in sight. Where could he
have got to? He shaded his eyes and examined the whole
length of the street, half a mile of it, sloping up to the
church and schools, the ochre-coloured houses tightly
shuttered; everything silent beneath the sun.

He began to walk up the street, peering up and down
every lane as he crossed it but seeing no sign of the
donkey. He was puzzled and began to wonder if, after all,
Federico might have run off into the country, unless he
had followed the road in the opposite direction and was
now on his way to the next village.

He was just beginning to think that he might as well
go back home and hope that Federico would do the
same, when he saw him. The main road led into a big
square plaza in whose centre was a covered market.
Three of its gates were shut but the middle one was open
and it was from just inside this centre gate that
Federico's rear end protruded.

His tail swished excitedly, a sign that he had undoubtedly found something invitingly edible, and, with a sinking feeling in his stomach, Antonio broke into a run, calling, 'Federico! Federico!'

Federico had indeed found something good to eat. The old lady who sold bales of lucerne and straw and dry animal fodder had been fast asleep when first he discovered her stall beside the open market door. He dipped his muzzle into the open sack of bran, then into one of maize, and then he discovered the lucerne, which was the most delicious thing he had ever tasted, soft, juicy and sweet-scented.

The bales were tied tight with string and he had to pull and shake them to get a decent mouthful. In the process, all the bales came tumbling down, almost on top of the old woman's head. She woke with a start, let out a

shriek of astonishment, and it was at this moment that Antonio arrived on the scene.

'So! What's this?' she cried, grabbing his shoulder. 'Taking advantage of an old woman's sleep to steal from her.'

'It's not true,' cried Antonio, trying to wriggle free, but she dug her hard nails into him, making him wince.

'Look! Look! Look at the mess he's made.' With each word her voice grew sharper. 'How long have the pair of you been here?'

Still holding on to Antonio, she pulled open the little drawer in the table where her scales were, half believing that he might have stolen her money too. Meanwhile Federico went on chewing unconcernedly a fresh mouthful of lucerne.

'Get hold of him!' cried the woman, giving Antonio a push. 'Don't let him eat any more.'

Antonio was at a loss as to how to hold him because Federico had managed to lose the bridle and just shook himself free when he dragged on the rough bit of mane between his ears. Then he snatched another mouthful of lucerne, breaking open a new bale as he did so. There were tears in Antonio's eyes and his lower lip trembled.

The woman grabbed her broom and was about to set on the pair of them when a passing farmer interrupted.

'Why don't you put a bit of string round him?' he suggested. 'You can't expect the boy to hold him with nothing.'

'Get the Guards,' screeched the woman. 'I'm not letting either of them go from here until someone's paid me for all the damage they've done. Where's your father?' she snapped at Antonio, her dark eyes witch-like in her fury. 'I'll make sure he gives you a good beating for this.'

'It wasn't my fault,' Antonio began in a shaky voice. 'The donkey ran away. I tried to catch him but I couldn't find him.'

'That's nothing to do with me. I want to know who's going to pay the damage.'

As it happened, the two Civil Guards of the village were in the tavern just across the road. The farmer had just come from there and went back to fetch them.

It all seemed a terrible nightmare to Antonio as he watched them officiously approach, the sort of thing that could only happen while he was asleep, when imagination ran riot. Everybody was afraid of the Civil Guards because throughout their history, ever since they had been first introduced to rid the countryside of bandits, they had been renowned for their severity and, although there were no longer any bandits to be captured, alive or dead, their image was for ever tarnished.

The sun glinted on their squat, patent-leather hats and pistol cases as they crossed the road into the shadow of the market place. One of them unbuttoned a breast pocket and pulled out a small notebook while the other one asked, 'What's going on here? What's all the fuss about?'

First the farmer explained what he understood of the situation, then the old woman, not satisfied with interrupting him half a dozen times, gave her version of the story. Afterwards Antonio, hardly able to speak, explained in a halting whisper how he had been trying to teach Federico to accept his commands.

'What's the extent of the damage?' asked the guard, who was making the notes.

'At least fifty pesetas,' the old woman claimed.

Antonio thought he would die.

'Come now,' said the guard. 'I think he could hardly have eaten fifty pesetas worth of grain and lucerne in such a short time.'

His companion was looking into the sacks and pushing the fallen corn about with his foot.

'He's ruined six bales of lucerne. I can't sell it now, even though it's not all eaten.'

'At three-fifty the bale, that's twenty-one pesetas,' said the farmer implacably.

'What about the bran? Look at it, spilled all over the ground!'

'At six pesetas the kilo. There's not half a kilo there.'

'And the maize?' She wouldn't give up.

'Say six pesetas the lot.'

'What about all the cleaning up I shall have to do? I'm an old woman. Besides, I had an awful fright when all those bales fell on top of me. I'm trembling all over.'

She proferred a skinny, wrinkled arm which was indeed trembling, but probably with indignation.

'We'll say thirty pesetas,' said the guard, not even looking at her arm. 'I reckon that's fair. Now, my lad, where do you live?'

Antonio hung his head and bit his lip. It would be terrible when his parents learned of the trouble Federico had caused. And thirty pesetas! The tears plopped to the ground amid the scattered purple lucerne flowers, where Federico was still nuzzling and stamping his sharp little hooves.

'Come on, boy,' he repeated sharply. 'Where do you live?'

The guard had the same accent as his parents. He must have come from the same part of Spain. He was a 'foreigner' too.

He wiped the back of his hand across his nose and found the courage to look up. For a second some of his fear had receded, just because the accent had the comforting sound of his own people. But the only expression on the man's face was one of growing annoyance at Antonio's tardiness in answering.

He gave his name and address and meanwhile the farmer tied a bit of string round Federico's neck. He put the end of it into Antonio's hand.

'Be careful he doesn't escape again,' he warned, giving a wink. 'He might get you into more trouble next time.'

'Bah!' exploded the woman. 'These foreigners. They don't know how to bring up their children. I'd better not see you round here again or else . . .'

Miserably Antonio walked his donkey back home. Now that Federico had done his worst, he was content to walk quietly beside the boy, mulling over the few bits of lucerne stuck between his teeth. Every now and then he pushed his muzzle into Antonio's ribs, nipping the shirt and sometimes nipping the boy's skin. The prickles in his back started smarting again, and he pushed the donkey roughly away.

He couldn't love Federico just then, his heart choked

with dread. What would happen? What would his parents say? So far the only mischief Federico had got into had been about their own house and orchard, but now the Civil Guard would come to claim the thirty pesetas from his father, and perhaps admonish him for allowing a child to be in charge of an uncontrollable donkey. All the neighbours would see them!

Why couldn't he just sink into the ground and disappear for ever, rather than bring such shame to all his family.

He tied Federico up in the orchard and when he went away without any of his usual caresses, Federico pricked his ears and stared after him, braying with surprise, perhaps trying to ask Antonio what was wrong. But the boy's head was bowed and he didn't look back.

Federico watched him for a moment more then he began nibbling at the bark of the almond tree before reaching up in a vain attempt to get at some of the leaves.

*

Much to Antonio's astonishment, his father was not so angry about the affair as he had expected. He was angry with the woman in the market place, who had made so much fuss about nothing, and said so to the guards in a loud voice so that the eavesdropping neighbours could hear.

Antonio he only lightly admonished, saying, 'But why didn't you tell me before about the trouble you're having with the donkey?'

'I didn't want to because Mama is always saying he's a

good-for-nothing, and me too. I wanted to show everyone that we're not.'

His father laughed and pinched his cheek. 'All donkeys are pig-headed. It shows they're intelligent and know how to think for themselves. We'll just have to take him in hand a bit, that's all.'

'You're going to help me, then?' Antonio's eyes shone with contentment. He could hardly believe it.

'You want him to win the races, don't you? You're not going to let those Mallorquines get all the prizes, are you?'

Everyone except María went to the orchard to watch Señor Torres and Antonio put Federico through his paces. Antonio was on his back and his father held a firm grip on the halter beneath the donkey's chin.

When he wanted him to start he clicked his tongue and cried, '*Arré, arré!*' and set off at a run, pulling Federico along beside him. When he wanted him to stop he commanded more softly, '*So–o!*'. It was a long-drawn-out sound, quite distinct from the sharp order to move, and Federico's stiff, twitching ears showed that he was listening to everything.

Shadows lengthened beneath the trees as he trotted up and down, up and down, with Antonio bouncing about on his back.

'Try to hold on tighter with your knees,' shouted Señor Torres.

Antonio tried and found that he didn't bounce about half so much, but he still felt as though his teeth would be shaken out of his mouth, together with quite a few other bits of him.

Soon Antonio tried the commands. His father had other things to do and, besides, the donkey was the boy's responsibility. While the trees melted into the darkness and the sky and mountains became one deep shadow, he rode Federico alone round the borders of the orchard, walking now because both he and the donkey were tired.

His brothers had given up watching. Their voices echoed from a distance, high-pitched, excited and quarrelsome. Marieta still kept him company, crouched on the ground and leaning her back against the pigsty, hardly able to keep her eyes open.

At last Antonio was satisfied. He slipped from the donkey's back, aching all over from the jogging he had received. He found he could hardly walk. His legs didn't seem to belong to him at all and it needed all his concentration to put one foot in front of the other. He was overwhelmed with joy and gratitude because his donkey had learned so quickly what was required of him, but Federico himself didn't seem to think that he had been particularly clever.

The donkey race

Federico didn't forget the lessons he had been taught. Once he knew what was wanted of him, he was reasonably obliging. Antonio found it was quite unnecessary now to use the saw-ridged bridle. Even without a halter round his head or any reins to guide him, he had only to call, '*Arré!*' or '*So–o!*' and Federico would either start or stop.

It was a bit more difficult to make him go to the right or the left or to turn right round, but by the time the day of the races arrived Antonio felt more or less satisfied that his donkey would at least be able to dash from the start to the finish without any special assistance on his part, except perhaps a few shouts or thumps with his heels in encouragement.

On the day of the races it was very hot. It was hot all the time in the summer, but on that particular afternoon the sky seemed to be trembling under the pressure of so much heat and neither people nor animals felt like doing anything but doze and keep still.

A farmer had agreed to lend one of his fields for the race meeting and, although it had the advantage of length and space, it was almost bereft of shade. The ground was stony and white, reflecting the heat, and the carob trees were a good hundred yards from the centre of the field where the races were to be held.

By five o'clock hardly anyone had turned up. Antonio was the only one there with a donkey, surveying the field which was mostly inhabited by small groups of children who wandered from place to place. By six o'clock four more donkeys had arrived and, of these, three were elderly, their skin worn to bare patches by ill-fitting harness. Only one was as young and sprightly as his Federico, and he was a big colt, ridden by a teenage boy who kept a tight rein on the bit that jagged in his mouth and stung him with an almond switch whenever he began to get excited.

Antonio watched this animal with some admiration. Undoubtedly as beautiful as his own Federico, his legs were longer and more solid, and he was so full of nervous energy that by looks at least he was the obvious favourite.

Federico was very placid in comparison. Arrayed only in the old halter that he wore every day, with a bit of strong cord knotted on each side of the nose-band, he took in all the new sights and sounds with surprising calm. His ears and nose quivered at the scent of the other animals, but the heat was such that he cared more about finding a shadow than rubbing muzzles with the strangers.

There were five mules of varying sizes, ridden by farmers and boys, and there were two horses who were galloped bareback round and round the field by their masters, regardless of the heat, and whose flying hooves set even Federico on edge from time to time.

There was absolutely no organisation. Antonio hadn't known what to expect, but he thought that at least there would have been some post or string or a mound of stones to mark the starting and finishing lines. But there was just the field, across whose nakedness hardly anyone cared to wander. A few adults milled desultorily near the trees and a number of cars and motor-bikes were parked in the best bits of shade.

In spite of the bills posted all about the village—which had neglected to give the actual hour of commencement, perhaps because the organisers hadn't decided when to commence when the posters were printed—very few people attended. The mayor was there, dressed in his best suit and looking very uncomfortable, and with him were several advisers, looking important with a few papers in their hands and consulting their watches from time to time.

Juan, Miguel, Alberto and Marieta deserted their brother in favour of the races that were being organised for the children. They suddenly realised that these were taking place when a whole group of boys and girls went dashing across in the field in a yelling muddle.

The prize for the winner was an *ensaimada*, a light, crispy pastry, sweet with icing sugar, which was so delicious that it was even sent abroad in air-mailed boxes, although on the island it was what most people had for their breakfast, washed down with a cup of coffee.

There was so much quarrelling about who had won and who had cheated and who hadn't had a fair chance that an *ensaimada* was eventually offered to every competitor, to keep them quiet, and because, with such a heat, they were all drying up anyway and would soon be too hard to chew. There were a few more races, but no one felt much like running and interest in them soon petered out.

Then the two horses were raced against each other. Everyone in the field drew round to watch this event which promised to be the most exciting of the afternoon, as both horses were rearing, jumping and dancing about with nervous impatience.

They raced neck and neck from the bottom of the field to the top, stones flying from under their hooves, foam spattering from their jaws. One stopped dead and threw its rider and, accompanied by squeals and shouts from the spectators, careered off across the adjoining meadow with no intention of being caught. It was a spectacular end to the race.

Meanwhile the five mules and their seven riders were jogging down to the bottom of the field from where their race was to begin. Antonio watched with more concerned interest. Mules were more like donkeys and he was curious to see how they would behave.

They all set out at a trot, big, steady, unruffled animals, dark with sweat, most of them wearing the heavy bridles of their workday harness, complete with blinkers. The one with the collar broke into a canter and the others followed suit. The pace-maker then changed to a gallop, encouraged by the two boys on his back, one beating his neck, the other his rump, and by the time the rest had been urged to a similar pace it was too late for them to catch up. The big strawberry-roan mule, with the two boys up and the big collar almost hiding them from view, was the winner.

Then it was the donkeys' turn. Antonio looked anxiously about to see if any of his family would be watching. Marieta and Juan were up near the top of the field, but the other two had gone to watch the clay-pigeon shooting which was just about to start. His mother hadn't bothered to come. She had said she might if she finished her washing in time but there was no sign of her. He was glad, really, because he didn't know how Federico would behave, but he wished that his father could have come.

The five donkeys spread out more or less in a line. The starter looked them up and down, then he beckoned to Antonio.

'Come forward a bit,' he said. 'Your donkey's the smallest, so he ought to get a head's start on the rest.'

Federico obligingly began to move forward, but then he didn't want to stop and the man had to run after Antonio and help turn him round. The other colt began to play up, made nervous by the endless delay of everything, and meanwhile Federico looked from side to side, trying to gaze back at the donkeys behind him, perhaps wondering why he had been put in the lead and not particularly liking it.

Antonio bit his lips with nervousness and tried to keep himself calm by smoothing Federico's neck with his hand. The sun burned down on his head and even Federico's furry neck was hot to the touch.

Suddenly the word was given and all the donkeys set off at a smart pace. All that is except Federico. He stood quite calm, deaf to Antonio's shouts, watching all the other donkeys forge ahead but feeling in no way obliged to copy them.

Tears of rage and chagrin loomed in Antonio's eyes and he drummed the donkey with his heels.

'Come on, Federico! They're going to win. All of them. Don't just stand there. Come on!'

Federico twitched his ears, and whether he sensed the anxiety of his master's voice or whether he felt that he might be left out of something edible if he stayed behind, he suddenly broke into a trot, almost jerking Antonio off his back in his urgency.

The other donkeys were halfway up the field by the time Federico set out. There was no way of winning now and Antonio felt like pulling out of the race before he should hear everybody laugh at him. Miguel and Alberto had come running back and he could hear their jeers as they pointed at him.

'Arré, arré!' they shouted to Federico, their voices shrill with scornful laughter, and the little donkey was startled.

Perhaps he suddenly remembered the times they had teased him, perhaps he just wanted to get away from them, or perhaps it was just at that same moment that he realised those other donkeys were going to get at whatever they were after before him.

Whatever it was, he gave a squeal and a jump and lashed ahead as if a mad dog were at his heels. His whirlwind approach frightened one of the donkeys right off the course and the man pulled in vain to turn him round.

He overtook two more donkeys and the only one ahead of him, swift but steady, was the big and nervous colt, at which the lad began to beat just as soon as he realised that Federico was on his tail.

The sound of the switch frightened Federico. It smacked down almost under his nose and he jerked forward in a startled effort to escape it.

'Get out of the way!' yelled the lad on the big donkey,

63

pushing at Antonio with his foot.

Antonio hung on grimly, although he was frightened and could feel himself irretrievably slipping. He dug his nails into Federico's thick beige fur; he tried to find some grip with his knees, though this was impossible now with his nose bumping on the donkey's withers. But there were only a few yards to go. He just couldn't fall off yet!

He couldn't fall off, but he did. One second he was spreadeagled across the donkey's back and the next he was on the gound, rolling under the hooves of the other donkey right behind him. There were shouts and a scream, legs and hooves all over him and the rank smell of donkey in his nose. Then he found himself in someone's arms, dizzy, breathless, not even knowing if he was hurt, but shaking all over.

'Are you all right?' a voice was saying. 'Are you hurt?'

'And my donkey? My donkey?'

Blood ran from his nose and the man who had grabbed him pushed his head back. There was a crowd of people round him now, their faces blurred by the sun which burst into his eyes like daggers. They made him lay down, they dabbed at him with handkerchiefs and

64

bewildered him the more with their noise and movements.

Suddenly he was aware of Marieta crying and he sat up, calling to her.

She flung herself on top of him, screaming, 'Antonio! Antonio! You're not dead. You're not dead,' and she sat on his chest and burst into tears.

'Of course not,' he said gruffly, struggling back to a sitting position and pushing her off his chest. 'What about Federico?'

'I don't know. Someone's looking after him, I think.'

After a while Antonio's nose stopped bleeding and he was allowed to get up. There was a deep weal on the back of his hand, where the donkey's hoof had caught him and which was only now beginning to throb.

'Did I win?' he asked his sister. 'What happened?'

'Yes, you won. You fell off just as I was about to step forward, about half a length ahead of the other donkey.' It was one of the mayor's assistants who answered.

'I didn't fall off too soon, then? It was all right?'

'Just.'

'And Federico?' he asked again, wondering if the little donkey would be frightened by all that had happened.

But Federico was tied to a car bumper beneath one of the carob trees, swishing his tail to keep the mosquitoes at bay, quite unperturbed by the fuss and excitement of the race-course.

The mayor himself presented Antonio with the prize: a giant-sized *ensaimada* in a big, cardboard box, about the biggest Antonio had ever seen, at least two feet in diameter. There was also a silver coin of twenty-five pesetas, more money than he had ever had in his life, so in spite of his blood-spattered shirt and aching hand he was the happiest boy alive.

*

Thunder rolled and lightning flashed over the little house that night and soon the rain was streaming in torrents over the roof-tops and dripping its dancing tune through the leaks in the tiles.

The children sat about the table in the kitchen while Antonio carefully lifted the lid from the huge round box, and a gasp of anticipatory delight escaped five mouths simultaneously at the sight of the gleaming brown pastry

66

nestled within a border of laced white paper and speckled all over with icing sugar.

Juan licked his lips and Marieta sighed with satisfaction. It was almost a pity when Antonio took the knife and began to cut into it.

No one took any notice of the storm and the cracking thunder, not even Federico who was watching from the open stable door. He would have ventured right into the kitchen, had not María been there setting out the plates and serviettes, but everyone was in such a happy mood that night that even she might have raised no argument had he pushed his way in and waited patiently at the table for a share to be set out for him too.

First communion

When Antonio was eleven years old Marieta was seven and Federico was two. There was nothing very special about being eleven, and Federico, of course, knew nothing of age. He was still a colt, a frisky, self-willed handful, even for Antonio who was well accustomed to his ways.

For Marieta, however, there was something very special about being seven years old. She had been looking forward to this particular birthday ever since her mother had told her, 'As soon as you're seven you'll be able to receive your first communion, and on that day you'll be the prettiest girl in all the village.'

María could hardly be blamed for spoiling her daughter. After four sons she had just about given up hope of ever having a baby girl, which was all she had really wanted from the beginning. Her brothers didn't really mind about her being spoiled. They were used to having her made more of than any of them. Besides, she was the baby of the family, and everyone knew that girls were sissies anyway.

Ever since Marieta's birth María had looked forward to the day of her first communion. It was the most important day in the life of every child in Spain and for girls especially so, second only to their future wedding day. So María had been planning for years just what her daughter would wear and who would be invited to the customary celebration. Expense was no object. Although she was a frugal woman by necessity and upbringing, the idea of scrimping money for such an important event didn't even occur to her.

For the whole of a year she had been saving money, ever since the nuns had told her that Marieta could read and write and knew the catechism by heart. But even so it wasn't enough. She worked harder every day, washing, sewing and scrubbing for everyone who needed some assistance, and nagged at her husband constantly because he wouldn't let her take a job in the tourist hotels where everyone knew that such a lot of money could be earned.

By the time the date for the communion was decided upon, at the beginning of May, there was still not enough money to pay for all that was needed. The fancy cakes which the baker was making specially on the day itself, the drinks, the ice-cream, the best smoked ham.

'Give them a few olives and a glass of beer and be done with,' snapped Señor Torres, when María went on and on about the price of everything.

He was very much against such extravagance, but, for once, had to give way. He refused to take part in any of the preparations and spent the evenings digging in the orchard, sighing over the price of vanity.

One terrible evening over the supper table María suddenly stated, 'We'll have to sell that donkey.'

'Who? Federico?' Antonio couldn't believe his ears.

'Who else? He's no use to us, eating his head off in the orchard and doing nothing to earn a living.'

'But the boy loves him,' defended Señor Torres. 'Why sell him if it's not necessary?'

'It is necessary. We shall need at least another three

thousand pesetas to pay for Marieta's dress and shoes and everything.'

'You still haven't enough!' he exploded, and the children shrank in expectation of another quarrel.

'You don't realise how much things cost these days, and I'm not having my daughter looking less than all the others.'

'Surely she could borrow someone else's dress and shoes.'

'You should be ashamed! Your only daughter, and you want her to wear someone else's dress and shoes for the most important occasion of her life!'

'But it's only one day. At least Antonio's outfit has been used by all the boys in turn.'

'And shabby they looked too. I won't have people saying we can't afford to buy a communion dress for Marieta. You'll just have to sell the donkey.'

Antonio looked at his father, his eyes expressing his desperation. Surely he wouldn't give in? Surely a dress for Marieta, which she would wear only once in her life, couldn't be as important as Federico.

'I wouldn't get three thousand for him. I'd be lucky to get half that.'

His tone was half-conciliatory. Even he had pride, as far as his children were concerned. Antonio dropped his gaze, his eyes pricking with tears he didn't want anyone to see.

'Get on with your meal,' he suddenly shouted at them all, seeing how they all stared and let the soup grow cold, and all but Antonio were startled into action.

Antonio couldn't eat. His throat, his heart, were

swollen with dread. Not even the slippery vermicelli could go down and a tear plopped into the soup as he fiddled with his spoon in a pretence of eating.

He couldn't imagine life without Federico. The donkey was everything to him, a brother, a friend, almost a mother in some ways because Federico enjoyed nuzzling and rubbing all over him, just as if he were bestowing the kisses and affection that Antonio's mother never had time for. His father's words broke in upon his thoughts.

'I'm only thinking of the boy. You know how he loves that donkey.'

'Bah!' scoffed María. 'He's too old for such childishness. It's about time he realised what life's about. Always dreaming over that animal's ears. He forgot to go for the milk yesterday and this morning he dropped a whole bottle full of oil in the lane. Then you wonder where the money goes!'

'You expect too much of him. He's only a lad.'

'At his age you were working.'

'You're a hard woman,' sighed her husband at last. 'You're determined to have your way.'

'I've never heard so much fuss about the sale of a donkey. One would think we were selling a child.'

'Antonio's crying,' piped up Marieta. 'Please don't sell Federico.'

'You want to have a lovely dress, don't you? You want to be as pretty as all your little friends?' her mother reminded.

Marieta nodded agreement, then added, 'But I don't want you to sell Federico. Why not sell the other donkey?'

71

'Because we wouldn't get the same price for her. She's old and no good for hard work any more.'

'Could she have another baby, for Antonio?'

'I expect so.' It was an easy consolation.

'I don't want another one,' muttered Antonio, his voice thick with emotion. 'What's the point, if you're only going to take it away from me?'

As soon as he could get away from the table, he went to see Federico, who was dozing in the orchard, twitching his muscles to frighten the mosquitoes off his withers and slapping the flies off his haunches with his tail.

He was so beautiful, the colour of milky coffee, with a white muzzle and trim, dark little hooves, and he pricked his ears with such anticipation as Antonio came towards him. The boy couldn't believe that Federico could ever be anywhere except here beneath his favourite almond tree, waiting for him, the sun through the leaves making dappled shadows on his haunches.

He couldn't think of anything to say to Federico that evening. His mind and heart were completely numbed, and his throat ached too much for even the customary words of greeting. He just rubbed him between the ears and let Federico nibble at his palm, and it didn't seem as though the world would ever be the same again.

*

It was Mestre Pedro who bought Federico. He and Antonio's father haggled for half a morning over the price of the donkey and at last the old farmer shook his head with a sigh of defeat and paid over a fair enough price. The donkey was young and strong, sparkling with vitality. There were no harness galls upon him and his lungs were as sound as his legs. It would be hard to find a finer donkey in all the village and Mestre Pedro knew it.

A few days later Antonio and Marieta took the early-morning bus with their mother into Palma to buy all the things that were needed. Antonio would have stayed behind. Once the trip to Palma would have been a thing of great excitement, almost an adventure, but now there was nothing that could bring a grin of anticipation to his tight-pressed lips or the light of excitement to his dark, sullen eyes.

He knew he was only needed to help carry all the packages. It was Marieta's day, the day on which she would try on the special white dress for the first time, choosing the prettiest and most expensive in the shop;

the white shoes and gloves and a lacy veil to cover her head, just like a bride. Then they went to a bookshop to buy a special white prayer book with a silver clasp, a rosary with white beads, and decide upon the invitation cards which would be specially printed.

There was no end to the list of things required and which could now be bought in exchange for Federico.

A week before the communion María began to white-wash all the rooms. She polished the floors and the furniture, she varnished the big black beams of all the ceilings, and throughout the days the sideboard in the kitchen began to fill with the gifts which different friends and relations brought for Marieta.

She couldn't touch any of the presents until the communion was over. Everything was on show, from the doll in its cellophane box dressed in a white communion dress just like her own, to the coloured pencils and satchel, the wrist-watch, the ankle socks and story books and silver charm bracelet.

No one else in the family had celebrated such a splendid communion, they hadn't been able to afford it before, and everything seem designed to taunt Antonio with the loss of Federico.

Everyone was happy and excited. Even Señor Torres was more cheerful now, looking forward to the extrava-gant feast and the dance that would come afterwards. He had an old record-player which was brought out two or three times a year, together with a dusty stock of the fox trots and tangos of his youth. In the past Antonio had always enjoyed helping him sort out the records and playing the old favourites over again, but now even the gay music echoed falsely in his pain-stricken heart.

Marieta was pallid with nervousness on the great day itself, unable to stop shaking while her mother dressed her in all the finery. She looked like a princess in her flouncy net and lace, with her dark hair pulled into stiffly lacquered ringlets on top of her head, over which the veil was carefully pinned.

She didn't cheer up and stop feeling sick until the ceremony at the church was over and the photographs had been taken, after which she was allowed to dispense with her veil and prayer book and rush about with the rest of the children, eating and drinking whatever they fancied.

The walls of the house resounded with shouts and laughter which spilled over into the yard and the lane, where people were gathered in groups; grandparents, relations and friends, neighbours and whoever else happened to stop by at the open door, and very few people had time to notice Antonio's listlessness.

Someone cried, 'What's the matter with Antonio?' and when María answered, 'He's sulking because we sold his donkey,' the person laughed and said, 'Get him a bike, then. That'll liven him up.'

Marieta was concerned about her brother. Of them all, she loved him the most, and, although she didn't feel as unhappy about Federico as he did, she very much wished that the donkey hadn't been sold because of her communion. It made it seem like her fault.

Some time in the evening, while they were watching the adults dancing, sitting halfway up the staircase because it was the only uncrowded place, she squeezed his hand and whispered, 'Don't worry, Antonio. You'll get Federico back, I know you will.'

'How?' he answered impatiently. 'I don't know how.'

'This morning, in church, I asked the Virgin to get him back for you. It was a very special prayer, so I'm sure She listened.'

Her eyes shone as she spoke, and, such was her certainty, that Antonio hadn't the heart to tell her that he didn't believe in miracles.

Mestre Pedro

Mestre Pedro lived in an ancient farmhouse about two miles from the village. The lane that led to his farm was no more than a cart-track which plunged between the undulating foothills of the pine and heather-covered mountains. He kept a few sheep and goats, he had a large mixed flock of chickens, ducks and turkeys, but his pride was in his orange groves, so neatly kept that from a distance they looked like a scene from a picture book instead of real life.

The rich dark soil was kept well turned; every leaf or twig or wayward fruit that fell from its tree was buried the selfsame day; every night the irrigation channels gurgled with water.

To help him with his labour a donkey was a most necessary work-mate, whether by pulling his plough and harrow, by patiently plodding in a circle to turn the big wooden wheel which brought up water from the well, or by carrying his produce to the village in the cart.

Mestre Pedro was a surly man, with little to say to anyone. He was accustomed to spending best part of the day alone, bent over his vegetables or his melons, and this was a silent job unless he felt like singing. But Mestre Pedro had never felt a song inside his heart and so he worked in silence, except when he grumbled aloud about the slow progress of his cabbages or tomatoes.

To him, Federico was just a tool of his trade, as necessary as a hoe or a saw or a pruning knife. He cared for him in the same way he would care for any tool, because careful treatment would make it last longer and Mestre Pedro never spent a peseta unless it was absolutely essential, but he felt no more for Federico than he would for any inanimate object in his possession.

His few words were short and sharp. Go! Stop! and occasionally the annoyed exclamation, Donkey! whenever Federico didn't quite do what he wanted.

Unfortunately, Federico quite often didn't do what was wanted because he had never been taught anything beyond the simplest commands. He knew nothing about pulling a cart or turning a water-wheel.

Mestre Pedro had a stick. All his life he had used a stick with donkeys without ever questioning its necessity. Donkeys rumps were made for beating, just like drumskins. He whacked him when he shouted 'Go', he whacked him when he shouted 'Stop', and he whacked him with every intermediate command.

He probably didn't mean to hurt him, any more than he expected to hurt the ground by walking over it. It had just never occurred to him that a donkey might not enjoy being walloped about thirty times a day. In fact, most donkeys got used to his ways and expected to be beaten as much as they expected to be fed.

Federico had never been beaten in all his two years. He had known only gentleness at Antonio's hands and hardly remembered the occasions when Miguel and Alberto had enjoyed throwing stones at him to frighten him.

The abrupt change from one home to another, the sudden loss of his dam, of Antonio, of all he had ever known, was extremely disconcerting, and for the first few days all he could do when he was left alone was wander round in circles, braying loudly and constantly for those he had lost.

Other donkeys answered him whose voices he did not recognise. He didn't know whom he missed more, the old, chocolate-coloured jenny who had ever been his companion and from whom he had still suckled in absent-minded moments, or Antonio who came running to him every evening with sugar or bread or a few nobs of maize in his hands.

When, after much difficulty and not without a certain amount of cursing, Mestre Pedro managed to back him into the cart and harness him up, he just stood and shook from ears to tail. A pair of floppy blinkers half cut off his vision, the unaccustomed collar weighed round his neck and withers like some monstrous beast that meant to suffocate him, and the rigid handlebars on either flank were of equally ominous intention.

He wouldn't move. He couldn't move. He was frozen to the spot with fear.

Mestre Pedro's eyes were more trained to observing fallen twigs, patches of mould and the movement of ants among his trees than the behaviour of donkeys, and the answer to any problem was in his hand. It was the straight branch of a tree, hard and as solid as a walking stick, whose bumps and knobbles had worn smooth on many a donkey's rump, and it came down on Federico's soft, plump hindquarters with a whack which frightened him as much by its noise as the pain it inflicted.

Mestre Pedro nearly fell off the cart as Federico suddenly dashed away, crazed with bewilderment and fear. He shouted for him to stop, pulling vainly at the reins which Federico didn't feel in his panic, and began using the stick with greater force, certain that this was the only remedy.

Federico didn't stop until he ran the cart up against a haystack and was jerked to his haunches. Then Mestre Pedro cursed and shouted and marched about with his stick in his hand until Federico was all to pieces with fear.

Mestre Pedro had never encountered such a donkey. Those he had kept before had all been used to carts and sticks and curses. He had a lot of things to do and in the end decided to leave Federico harnessed to the cart until he got used to the feel of it. He tethered him to a ring in the wall, his muzzle almost touching the stone, and marched away grumbling but already thinking of his oranges.

*

Federico never really learned what was wanted of him. He was so terrified of Mestre Pedro that he had only to hear or see the farmer coming towards him to start shaking all over. Soon he began to lay back his ears and lift a hindleg menacingly, in self-defence and because he was so frightened.

He never intended to do any harm. He still wasn't really aware of the power that was in his teeth and hooves, but in his fear he was driven instinctively to protect himself. Mestre Pedro was used to such tricks. He knew more about them than did Federico. He put a wire muzzle over his mouth and rapped his legs so sharply that Federico quickly realised he must keep his fear to himself.

He grew accustomed to the cart and the blinkers that flapped all the time; the collar no longer seemed so heavy and the handlebars ceased to be a menace. But his gait was always erratic, either too fast or not fast enough, part walk, part canter, part out-and-out bolt, because the stick was always behind him and his one idea was to escape it.

Mestre Pedro didn't connect one thing with the other. He only came to the conclusion that the donkey was crazy.

'A fine animal you sold me!' he exclaimed to Señor Torres when next he went to collect the rent.

'Why, what's the matter with him?'

'Scared of a cart! Scared of a shadow, if you ask me! What's the matter with him?'

'Perhaps you've gone the wrong way about teaching him. I told you he wasn't much broken, Mestre Pedro.'

'I've had donkeys since I was a boy. Fifty years now I've had donkeys and I've never had any trouble.'

'He's only a two-year-old. You need patience.'

'Patience! I haven't got time to waste. Time's money,' and, at this, he suddenly realised he was wasting time, now that he had the rent in his hands. So, with an abrupt 'Goodbye' he was on his way, shaking his head and still grumbling.

Federico worked very hard. His fat fell away and he grew lean and tough. Mestre Pedro's rough jerks at the bridle rubbed the skin off his soft grey muzzle. Flies crawled over the sores and drove him wild until they more or less healed into a hard scar which was only occasionally broken. The ill-fitting collar rubbed the hair off his withers and the stick flattened the hair on his rump. It was just as well that Antonio couldn't see him.

At night Federico was hobbled and left to his own devices in a lonely, hilly field from whose stony earth olive trees twisted in weird, prehistoric aspect. He was given a few forkfuls of lucerne, dried in the sun, the inevitable locust beans, and he would wander round nibbling at the weeds and thistles which struggled from under the stones.

He hated his loneliness and was afraid of the darkness that hid everything except the unfriendly shapes of the trees. His only consolation was in the sounds he knew: the staccato bleat of a disturbed ewe; a rush of barks; the bray of a distant donkey. This latter was rare indeed, for donkeys are silent animals mostly, who only give voice when they have something important to make a noise about.

Federico was silent after the first few days. He had called for his mother, he had called for the boy, he had called for all that he had known and lost; and when none of these things came back to him, he didn't call any more.

The battle

Antonio couldn't forget Federico. It was no use talking about him, at least not while his mother was in hearing, and even his father had lost interest in the subject. They were both well pleased with Marieta's communion, which had been as splendid as the neighbour's, and when it was over and life resumed its normal course—interrupted only by the arrival of the very expensive photographs, which gave further cause for excitement and pleasure— the absence of Federico wasn't noticed by anyone except the boy who loved him. Even the mother donkey didn't seem to care.

So Antonio didn't talk about Federico any more and tired of going down to the orchard, pretending that he might somehow be there if he kept a vigil for him. He was too old to be able to pretend like that for very long. But he did have another idea.

He would go and see Federico at Mestre Pedro's place. He wouldn't bother the farmer. He wouldn't ask any favours. He would just go to the farm with the hope of being able to see his donkey.

His heart leaped as the idea came to him. He only wanted to see him, after all. That would be enough to drive away the dull pain which had never left his heart ever since the donkey had been taken away.

It was a long way to Mestre Pedro's farm. The road wound uphill through the deserted pine-woods. The only sound was that of the cicadas, shrill, piercing and constant. Was it really possible that they made such a noise by rubbing their legs together? Magpies hopped over the pebble-strewn ground, the sun gleaming on their blue and black plumage. They were the only creatures that moved.

The sun burned down on the melting black road. Antonio's head began to ache and his eyes saw everything through a blur. At last he reached the cart track that turned towards the farm, the only sign that men ever went that way. Then, ten minutes later, having passed a place where the pine trunks were sawn off and piled beside the cart track, the first of Mestre Pedro's orchards came into view.

The hope he had nurtured of being able to slip over a wall in order to get close without being seen was quickly dashed. Mestre Pedro's fields were surrounded by well-tended strands of stiff barbed wire which topped a high wire mesh over which he couldn't possibly climb.

For an hour he wandered round the outskirts of the farm. His throat was parched with thirst and some pears that hung just beyond his reach were sorely tempting. There were plums, too, not far away and apricots ripening among big clusters of leaves, but Mestre Pedro had measured his fences to the last inch. The fruit remained tantalisingly close but out of reach. It was then that he heard voices.

Coming along the cart-track from somewhere in the hills beyond the farm were three boys and a donkey. One boy was dragging the animal along by the halter, another was beating at his rump with a stick, while the third sat on his back and banged him with his heels.

The boys were Mestre Pedro's grandsons and the donkey was Federico.

They didn't see Antonio, fully occupied by their efforts to keep the donkey in motion. Federico kept digging in his hooves, his ears back, his eyes wild, his hindlegs kicking out every few minutes. He was absolutely fed up with his three new masters and showing it as well as he knew how. The only reason they could keep him going now was because he was on the home stretch and he hoped for some respite, but he went in fits and starts, protesting all the way.

It was young Pedro who saw Antonio first. He was sitting on Federico's back and having the easiest time of it.

'Look who's here,' he called. 'The foreigner who had the donkey before.'

Tomeu, thirteen, bulky and as surly as his grandfather, stared threateningly at Antonio. 'What are you doing here? Stealing my grandfather's fruit, I suppose.'

'I came to see the donkey,' said Antonio, trying to sound braver than he felt.

'Well, now you've seen him, so get out of here. We don't want any foreigners hereabouts.'

Antonio stood his ground. He dared not turn his back or run. He didn't trust any of them. Suddenly Federico recognised him. His ears went up and his eyes lost their whiteness. He wrinkled up his nose and let out a hearty bray of greeting.

'Shut up!' shouted Tomeu, into whose ears most of the bray had gone, and he punched Federico in the face.

'Leave him alone!' cried Antonio, growing hot with indignation.

'It looks like this donkey and the foreigner understand each other,' laughed Joan, the boy with the stick. 'They probably speak the same language.'

'You don't need to hit him,' went on Antonio, not caring about the intended insult.

His fear was receding. He had forgotten that they could hurt him if they wanted to because they were hurting Federico.

'He'll do what you want without being beaten.'

'What do you know about it?' retorted Joan. 'Just because he was your donkey before, doesn't mean you can tell us how to treat him now.'

Federico was shaking his head, trying to get away from Tomeu, trying to get closer to Antonio. He brayed again and bucked. Pedro landed in the dust.

'Animal!' raged Tomeu, turning on the donkey

with all his brutish nature and beginning to hit him again with his fist.

Antonio couldn't bear any more. Caution was lost in the blaze of fury that choked his breast. He picked up the biggest stone he could find in the moment and threw it with all his might at Tomeu's head. Blood spurted as the boy staggered and fell, and Antonio stared incredulously. But only for a second because Pedro and Joan were already filling their hands with stones which they began to pelt after him as soon as he took to his heels.

He felt the bite of one just beneath his shoulder blade. Another whizzed past his head and bounced along the track ahead of him. Terror pounded inside him as he deserted the track in favour of the hillside, feeling safer as he dodged round the broad pine-trunks and scratched through the thorn bushes. His foot caught in a tuft of heather and he split his knees on the stony ground, but his pursuers were only a few paces behind and he hadn't time to feel any pain.

Thwack! A really heavy stone took the wind out of him as it thudded into his spine, and he stopped with a gasp. A few paces ahead was the stack of felled trunks. He just had to reach it though his head rocked and there wasn't a breath left in him.

One last effort and he was there, cowering as low as he could to the churned up earth and blinking the perspiration from his eyes. There were a few stones which he feverishly gathered beside him but he dared not look over the top of the logs in case his pursuers saw him.

He heard Joan call out, 'Can you see him?', and young Pedro answer, 'Looks like he got away.' Then Joan said

'We'd better get back to Tomeu. He was bleeding like a pig. Maybe he's dead by now.'

Tense and terrified, Antonio waited for them to go away. He dared not move until everything was absolutely still, except his heart which raced as fast as ever. Then he made a dash up the hill behind him and, on reaching the top, to his great relief he saw the asphalt road gleaming and black below him.

When he got down on to it the sobs burst out of him, delayed reaction to the fear and indignation that had almost burst his lungs and heart. He discovered his Sunday shirt and trousers torn and stained with dirt, his knees bleeding, a thorn stuck in his toe inside his sandal, and with every breath he took pain stabbed through his back.

He sobbed all the way along the road, without shedding a tear, a dry, empty, hopeless sound which only the magpies heard.

*

Everyone was asleep when he reached home except his mother, who was in the yard doing some washing. She gave a fierce cry at the sight of him, dragged the clothes off him with a flurry of slaps and pushes which did indeed bring the tears to his eyes, not because she hurt him—he was hardened to such treatment—but because it was more than he could bear after all he had been through. He needed someone to listen, to sympathise, to dispel his terrible fear about the harm he had done to Tomeu, but he couldn't get in a word between her outraged scoldings.

'Get in that tub!' she shouted, pointing to the big earthenware basin in which she washed both the clothes and the children. She scrubbed the sweat and blood off him with the same energy she used for the sheets and when he was drubbed clean, she sent him with a clout round the ear to look for his other clothes.

After that Antonio couldn't say where he had been or what had happened. He just couldn't say a word to anyone, not even to his father who asked questions with far more patience and without a hint of anger.

That night Mestre Pedro called at the cottage. Antonio heard his father and the farmer arguing with angry voices for quite some time. He was glad he had been sent to bed without any supper, and so escaped seeing Mestre Pedro, but he was trembling with dread as his father later came up the stairs.

Señor Torres sat on the bed and stared at his pale-faced, tight-lipped son. He looked more worried and upset than Antonio had ever seen him and he dropped his gaze in shame.

'Mestre Pedro says you threw a stone at Tomeu without any reason and split his head open. He lost a lot of blood and had to have five stitches in the wound.'

Every statement sounded like an accusation, bringing a surge of new bitterness to Antonio's heart. He couldn't even feel glad that Tomeu was only injured. He could only remember his indignation.

His father was waiting for him to say something so in a low voice he admitted, 'He was hitting Federico and I told him to stop.'

'You shouldn't have thrown the stone.'

'There were three of them. They threw stones at me too.'

'But you started it.'

Antonio's eyes flashed. 'They were hitting Federico.' It was his defence, but only to himself was it sufficient.

'What's that to do with you?' his father retorted impatiently. 'Or have you forgotten that the donkey belongs to Mestre Pedro now?'

Antonio pressed his lips together. If his father couldn't understand, what was the use of trying to explain? His father sighed and put a hand on his arm.

'I know you love him,' he began again, more gently this time. 'But you can't expect other people to love him too. A donkey is only a donkey. They get used to being knocked about. I bet you've had more whacks than Federico.'

Antonio looked at his father with a bewildered expression.

'Why did you sell him? He was the only thing I ever really wanted.'

'You shouldn't have set your heart on him so. It's wrong to love animals like people because they don't love us in the same way. I don't suppose he really misses you.'

'He called to me . . .'

'He would have called to his mother as well, had he seen her. He recognised you. It was no more than that.'

It was no good trying to make anyone understand. His feelings were contrary to everyone else's and therefore they were wrong. They would call him spoiled and childish, like his mother, or accuse him of crying for the moon, like his father. The donkey was sold and, as far as they were concerned, he just didn't exist any more. He was no more to them than the pig they had slaughtered the winter before.

There was a long silence and then his father said, 'I want you to promise me something. I want you to promise never to go near Mestre Pedro's place again. We can't afford to get into trouble with him. There's been enough trouble as it is. You're old enough to have realised that the people here don't really like us, so don't give them cause to complain. Forget about the donkey.'

He paused, waiting for Antonio to speak.

'Do you promise?'

'I promise not to go near Mestre Pedro's farm, but I can't forget the donkey.'

'He's not yours any more. Whatever happens to him has nothing to do with you. Just remember that and, when you're tired of moping over what you can't have, perhaps you'll start thinking about something else.'

Federico runs away

Mestre Pedro's grandsons spent most of their Sundays at the farm. During the holidays they were often there for days at a time and the new donkey was a great attraction for them. The previous one had been a mean old thing, sly as only a donkey can learn to be, but Federico was entirely different.

He was young and sturdy and full of energy and he didn't object too much at first when they got up on his back and rode him about the fields and lanes. It was the one thing he had been taught with patience and kindness, the one thing he really understood.

Federico soon learned that these boys weren't like Antonio. They had no patience; they had never been taught to treat an animal with kindness; they had no natural consideration. A donkey was only a donkey, tough, obedient, hard-working. You beat it to make it go and you beat it to make it stop, just as if it couldn't be put into gear without the aid of a stick.

The donkey quickly began to anticipate their approach with dread. When he saw them, or heard their voices, he hobbled to the far end of his field. He couldn't escape them and it was the only way in which he could protest.

They pulled his tail, they pulled his ears, they dragged him from one place to another, hurrying him one minute, restraining him the next, until he was too bewildered and fearful to know what they wanted. In fact, the boys didn't know either, except to enjoy themselves at the donkey's expense.

After a while he began using his heels, kicking out to keep them at bay. They retaliated with their sticks and soon overcame his resistance. His hooves were only small and he couldn't kick all three of them at the same time.

When Federico learned submission, life became less troublesome. There were things he just could not run away from, things he just could not beat, and the first lesson he learned was that resistance was the cause of all trouble and discomfort. He learned what all donkeys had to learn sooner or later, endurance, and he let Mestre Pedro's grandsons do as they wished, dumbly accepting their shouts and sticks and changeable whims.

When he'd had enough he just stopped dead, flattened his ears and refused to move. After that there was no way of forcing or convincing him and they usually left him alone. You couldn't move a tree, you couldn't move the very earth, and Federico made himself equally inanimate and unfeeling. They just had to give up.

When they went, when even their voices no longer rose stridently above the silent valley, Federico became a living thing again. He would drop his head in search of a thistle or a few blades of grass, ears waggling, tail switching at the flies, and it was as if the boys had never been there to torment him.

One afternoon, at the end of summer, when they had left him thus, frustrated by his absolute imperturbability, they forgot to hobble him before they went away. Federico didn't realise his legs were free until he began to use them and then he explored farther afield because movement was no longer a dragging, uncomfortable

94

process. He found a place where the wall had tumbled and if he scrambled across the scattered stones it was only because beyond them was a ridge, thick with wild corn and dandelions, whose existence Federico just couldn't ignore.

When he had browsed his way through most of this, he lifted his head, pricked his ears, and widened his nostrils, examining the new terrain with curiosity. The instinct to discover new places and things was always with him, in spite of the hobbles that discouraged unnecessary movement, and now that he was free his curiosity was irrepressible.

He nibbled across the entire length of the field, finding a few weeds between the stones and bits of grass here and there, but nothing really worth while, and he stopped at a rusted iron gate. For half an hour he just stood at the gate, nose lifted and quivering as the breezes that drifted down from the hills only a mile away, laden with pine and heather and the pungent scent of strange wild flowers, played about him.

Then he discovered that between the gatepost and the wall was a gap wide enough for him to squeeze through if he didn't mind scratching and trampling his way through the blackberry bushes trailing everywhere. He chomped off all the berries within reach and was then drawn to a solitary black fig tree whose fruit had burst and fallen to the ground, filling all the air with a sweet, heady odour.

Wasps, bees and bluebottles rose in a chorus of noise at his approach. Satiated flies glistened on the sunlit leaves, together with ants and other insects all claiming their share of the forgotten fruit. Federico waggled his ears and swished his tail, closing his eyes as he reached for the fruit on the lowest branches.

But he was driven away after only a few mouthfuls, snorting and trying to toss the wasps off his head as they stung and stung him. He cantered for quite a distance until fright faded, and when he stopped he looked back at the tree whose sweetness was still a temptation.

Then he caught the scent of more blackberries and was soon nosing through another jungle of brambles, equally content to snaffle leaves as well as fruit, the fig tree abruptly forgotten.

Bit by bit, without even realising it, Federico wandered farther and farther from his home field. Mestre Pedro's property had come to an end a long way back and he meandered along old pathways which showed no sign of belonging to anyone. There were a few tumbled walls here and there, but the countryside became progressively wilder as the mountains grew closer.

The sun had nearly gone. The hills ahead were almost in darkness while the fields behind glowed in its lingering rays. A dried-up water-course was a natural pathway through the steepening terrain. To all appearances it could have been a cart-track, except for the large boulders lying here and there which would have broken any axle.

Federico began to climb. The water-course, or torrent as it was called in those parts, was steep in places but mostly followed the natural curves in the hillside. There was no water and there rarely ever would be, except at a time of torrential rain or if snow should ever fall heavily on the mountains, as long ago it must have

done in order to form such lasting scars among the rocks and earth. He went on climbing until darkness fell and then he stopped because he could no longer see where he was going.

*

The following day Mestre Pedro discovered the donkey's disappearance. He couldn't understand what had happened until he found the forgotten hobbles still lying beneath the carob tree where his grandsons had thrown them. Then he searched all round the big, deserted field until he came across the broken wall, cursing all the time because he had a lot to do and was ever conscious of the passing minutes.

The boys had gone home or he would have sent them after the wandering donkey, and he mumbled angrily to himself about their carelessness.

He followed the donkey's trail as far as the fig tree, then stopped to glance at the spoiling fruit, irritated by the waste although it wasn't his tree. There was only one way the donkey could go from here, unless he deliberately strayed from the easiest paths, and, with a sigh of resignation, Mestre Pedro tackled the torrent which the night before had been trodden by Federico.

He climbed for a long time, looking for mushrooms on the way. There were clumps of toadstools in the mossy patches beneath the uncovered pine roots, some of which had been recently snapped and trampled, a fairly sure sign that the donkey had been there before him. So Mestre Pedro went on climbing, halting now and then to regain his breath and wipe the perspiration from his bald head with a grubby handkerchief.

He hadn't the energy to gaze much beyond his immediate surroundings or he would have seen the donkey far above him, watching his progress with intent curiosity.

Federico was standing on a huge rock which jutted out like a platform over the side of the mountain. The sun gleamed on him, its reach unbroken by hills or trees, and he had been standing there for some time, just gazing down on the vast sweep of countryside beneath him.

His pricked ears quivered with interest when he suddenly caught sight of the distant figure, toiling over rocks and tree-roots, and because he was still too young to have learned caution or guile, he uttered a loud bray of greeting.

'So there you are, you brute!' shouted Mestre Pedro, shaking his fist.

Federico brayed again, tossing his head up and down, then he shook himself and trotted off the platform, disappearing behind a holly bush. He had no intention of letting Mestre Pedro catch him.

It took the farmer another twenty minutes to reach the big rock itself and by then the donkey was nowhere in sight. He controlled his heavy breathing to listen for the sound of Federico's hooves but, unshod, they were noiseless.

'Where are you, animal?' he cried, his voice hoarse with exertion and rage.

Federico heard him and flattened his ears. He followed an upward trail, pattering swiftly along, confident in his new-found freedom, not even afraid that the farmer might catch him. There were no walls, no hobbles, no halter ropes to restrain him. The mountain was a free place and there he intended to remain.

Brought to bay

Mestre Pedro sent his grandsons to recapture Federico but they were equally unsuccessful. Then he didn't know what to do. The donkey seemed to have settled himself in the highest part of the hills, where grass was most abundant, but sooner or later he might go farther afield. The mountains were unfenced, riddled with sheep paths that ran in all directions, and there was nothing to keep Federico to one particular place.

It took him a week to think of something and then he went to see Señor Torres. He didn't like doing this because relations between them had been strained ever since the battle between Antonio and his grandsons. Señor Torres listened to his story politely but without much sympathy. When he had finished he asked, 'But what has it to do with me?'

'I thought your boy might be able to get him back for me. I remember you said they got on well together. Perhaps the donkey would come to him.'

Antonio was standing just behind the curtain in the doorway. He had heard Mestre Pedro talking about Federico, and although he knew it was impolite to listen to other people's conversations, he couldn't resist eavesdropping on this one. The farmer caught a glimpse of him and, almost too genially, asked, 'Do you think he'd come to you, lad?'

'Of course,' Antonio eagerly began, proud of all he had taught his donkey and only too glad to have the opportunity of seeing him again.

'Antonio!' His father checked him sharply, instantly subduing his sudden animation.

'Listen, Mestre Pedro. The last time you came here to talk about that donkey I remember you telling me—warning me, in fact—to keep my son away from him. Now it suits you to call another tune, but it doesn't suit me to dance to it.'

'But . . .'

'No buts. My son promised he'd keep away from the donkey and that promise still stands. The animal is yours. It has nothing to do with us. If you can't keep it, that's your affair. My Antonio isn't having any more to do with him.'

'Surely, under the circumstances . . .'

'I'm sorry, Mestre Pedro, but you can't expect me to worry about your animals. They're no concern of mine.'

The old farmer went away swearing and Antonio listened crestfallen while his father rated him for interrupting the conversation.

'I only wanted to get Federico back. I know he'd come to me. I'm sure he hasn't forgotten me.'

'And if you get him back? What then? It still doesn't make him your donkey and don't imagine that Mestre Pedro would be grateful. Leave him in the hills. There's plenty for him to eat up there and that's where he'll be happiest.'

Antonio was glad that Federico was free, glad that Mestre Pedro's grandsons could no longer torment him, but how it pained him to know that his donkey was up in the hills, free to come to him; that no one could prevent him caring for him once again, except his father who had forbidden it!

He believed that he had accustomed himself to living without Federico. There were times when he didn't even think about him. But now all the old feelings surged back. The love, the twist of pain, the dull ache of emptiness in his heart.

At suppertime he asked, 'If Federico were never recaptured, if he lived for years and years in the hills, would he still belong to Mestre Pedro?'

'I suppose so,' said his father. 'It's his donkey. He's got a licence to prove it.'

'But suppose he never caught him?'

'Well?'

'And someone else found him?'

'He'd still belong to Mestre Pedro.'

'But if that person kept him in the hills . . .'

'And why should he do that?'

Antonio shrugged. 'I don't know. Perhaps because . . .'

'If you're thinking you might be able to have the donkey back one day you'd better forget about it. The law is the law. Federico belongs to Mestre Pedro.'

There was silence for a while, except the usual sounds at mealtime, spoons scraping against the soup plates, bottle clinking against glass.

'Papa, do you think I could go to see Federico? Just to see him,' he rushed on as his father looked at him with impatience. 'I wouldn't bring him back to the village.'

'Antonio, you promised to leave the donkey alone.'

'I promised not to go to the farm.'

'It's the same thing. Leave him alone.'

'But if he's in the hills, free, like a wild animal . . .'

'Antonio!' The warning note in his father's voice silenced him at last, but, although he didn't speak any more, he continued to think.

There was no reasoning in his thoughts. There could be none while his heart wanted so badly. He just had to be near Federico once more, talk to him, scratch him between the ears, feel the soft lips mouthing his hands in search of sugar lumps. He believed he had forgotten all those feelings but they came back to him as if they had never been curtailed.

He planned to search for Federico the following Sunday, just as soon as he came out of church, and bought a whole box of sugar lumps with his pocket money in anticipation.

His idea was to keep Federico in a secret place, not too far from home. He would take the wood-axe with him to chop the lowest boughs from the pine trees to form a kind of corral. He would fill the fence with gorse to block up all the holes and Federico would always be there for him to visit as often as he could.

Ideas flooded him, each new one seeming better than its predecessor. If any doubts came to his head they were hurriedly brushed aside. All he cared about was having Federico again and, because his heart wanted so earnestly, everything was possible.

*

Antonio's plan didn't work. When Sunday came, some relations from Palma turned up, bringing presents for all the family. It was impossible to sneak away and he spent the whole day trying to disguise his impatience and disappointment. It was one of the longest in his life.

Meanwhile, that same Sunday, Mestre Pedro decided to make another attempt at getting the donkey down from the mountain. He had two hunting dogs, tall, lanky animals of ancient lineage, locally known as greyhounds, although their only likeness to the animal of the race-track was in their skeletal frames, tremendous speed and vicious nature. They looked more like the racing dogs of ancient Greece, one red, one red and white, hairy animals, whose quick noses and tireless pace were of unquestioned value in the hunting of hares and rabbits.

The dogs had been tied up for a long time and were uncontrollable in their excitement when Mestre Pedro came to unleash them. They snapped and snarled at each other, as dogs will when long confinement warps their dispositions, and the farmer lashed at them with his stick to keep them apart. They made a score of unnecessary journeys, back and forth, until their initial excitement was appeased and, by the time the hills were reached, were intent upon finding some kind of prey.

The air was close and sticky that Sunday morning. The sky was overcast with tempestuous clouds which had clogged round the highest reaches, unable to drag their heavy load across the peaks. Mist dawdled in pockets and clung to tufts of wiry grass.

Mestre Pedro could hardly breath. The dogs panted, their hollow flanks heaving, their long jaws flaying saliva in every direction. They whimpered and yelped in frustration because there was nothing they could chase.

At midday the farmer found a shady spot where he

could munch his bread and cheese and drink his wine. The dogs flopped themselves down in the coolest spot they could find and watched him. Soon he fell asleep. He didn't know how long the sleep lasted, but when he awoke the sky was considerably darker and there was a noise high in the hills which he didn't recognise until he had shaken the sleep out of his head. Then he knew the two dogs had found something. They were almost howling in their excitement.

He shouted out to them, but either they didn't hear him or their blood was up and they didn't take any notice. Had they found the donkey or was it a magpie or a lone rabbit?

The first drips of rain splashed in his face as he began to hurry, using his hands to pull himself over the rough places. Then the rain began to stream down, thudding over the earth and rocks as the drops grew larger, swifter and more numerous.

The dogs sounded as though they were going mad. Yelps, howls, barks, discordant and blood-curdling, which affected even Mestre Pedro with a sense of urgency. What was the matter with them? Perhaps they had fallen into a pothole and were clamouring to get out. The mountain was riddled with underground caves which claimed many a careless lamb.

Water streamed down the hillside now, gurgling between the stones. The dry mountain was suddenly one endless torrent, pushing pebbles and mud before it. If it hadn't been for the noise of the dogs, Mestre Pedro would have found some rock beneath which he could shelter. He could see almost nothing. His shirt was stuck

to him, the brim of his straw hat was a soggy mess that dipped in front of his eyes and his canvas shoes were filled with water.

He heard the donkey bray, a wild, desperate sound which stopped him in his tracks. The dogs must have found him, after all. Accursed rain which beat against him! If he didn't find the animals soon, it would be too late.

The rain didn't halt the dogs. The hunting instinct had set their blood on fire. They were two savage creatures, able to slash a sheep's jugular vein with a snap of their teeth or leave a hare paralysed with one bite through the neck. Any live thing on the mountain was theirs if they could catch it.

Federico knew next to nothing about dogs. They had never troubled him and he had no particular reason to be afraid of them. But the moment these two red and white animals came upon him, with a ferocious song in their throats, fear sent him flying away from them.

Had he been a sheep or a goat they would have pulled him down within a few minutes, to maul him at will and leave him kicking in the throes of death. But Federico was bigger than his attackers and the pursuit was more drawn-out. Racing beside him, they slashed at his flank and withers, tore at his fetlocks, hung on to anything they could grasp.

Federico turned on them at last, lashing with his hooves, using his teeth where he could, and for a moment the dogs drew back panting, their wide jaws stretched into a wicked grin, their yellow eyes appraising every part of him. Then they went for him again, undaunted by his show of courage, and the blood that began to show through the beige fur excited their ravening spirits the more.

The two dogs seemed like a dozen, attacking him from every side, swirling with waving tails and open jaws, merciless, blood-lusting, determined to kill. But he broke from their attack and fled a second time, fear-crazed, unaware of the rain. The sure little hooves carried him across rocks and soggy ground. Never had he run with such swiftness before, but the dogs kept to his flanks and made constant attempts at his throat.

One of them pulled up with a yelp of pain, his paw pierced by a thorn, and although he was soon in the chase again, running on three legs, it was too late for him to make up the lost ground.

With only the red and white dog in pursuit, Federico turned in desperation to face him. The two animals collided, fell over each other and rolled down the hillside together, the dog yelping raggedly. His back was broken and all he could do was howl and bite at the terrible pain while the donkey plunged away between the trees.

The first dog limped back to Mestre Pedro and it took him an hour, while the rain still fell, to find the other. There was no point in taking him home, he could see that straight away, so he finished him off and plodded back to the farm with only the red dog limping at his heels.

In the evening he went to the tavern to watch a football match on the television. He talked about the day's experience and the dog he had lost and, although he had gone by the time Antonio's father came in for a drink, the story was related anew.

Thus it was that Antonio learned about it too. His father told him how the dogs had been hurt, but no one seemed to wonder if Federico might have been injured too, except Antonio.

That night, the rain beating steadily over the tiles became a tattoo of fear in his heart, driving away sleep. He remembered how Federico had almost died on a similar rainy night, not so very long ago, and how he had only survived because he had been there to give him courage. This time Federico was alone and the mountain was a dark, dark place and comfortless.

Alone in the hills

Antonio fell asleep at last, but his fears were carried forward into his dreams. Monstrous dogs howled and whimpered throughout his unhappy slumber and all the time there was the terrible awareness that the donkey needed him, and he could not reach him. When he awoke, his bedclothes on the floor and his pyjamas soaked with perspiration, the grey light filtering through the shutters told him it was morning. The rain had stopped but the signs in the sky told of more to come.

The earth in the orchard smelled damp and sharp and the tree-trunks were a vivid black. Everything was clearer in colour and detail after the rain. Antonio's eyes scanned the hills beyond the orchard. They looked solidly green from here, with the occasional dark shadow of caves in the rock-face. Was Federico somewhere up there? Was it possible to find him now, after all that had happened?

Antonio could no longer distinguish between the news his father had given him and the anguish he had passed in his dreams. His whole being was tortured by fears for Federico and while he tore at his bread, hardly aware of Marieta chattering in his ear and his brothers shouting at each other, only one thought possessed him: to find the donkey as soon as possible and make sure he was safe.

He left Marieta at the convent and, as soon as his brothers were diverted, slipped out of the school playground and made towards Mestre Pedro's farm. He ran most of the way, bypassing the farm and making as directly as he could towards the hills. By this time there was no breath left in his lungs and he had to slow down.

The easiest way to climb the mountain was by following the torrent, which was more like a stream that morning with little pools of water caught between the big stones. Water trickled through all the cracks in the summer-dry earth and his rope-soled sandals were soggy with mud.

He looked for hoofprints all the way but saw none. There was no sign of Mestre Pedro's passing. The rain overnight had washed everything away. But he kept on climbing upwards knowing that sooner or later he would find his donkey. He had to. He just couldn't go home until he found him.

He found the dog first and flinched from looking at it. But at least he knew he must be on the right trail and was animated. He didn't know what time it was. His tired legs and the rumbling sounds in his stomach told him it was time for a rest and something to eat, but he had brought no food with him and he couldn't afford to stop for a while.

Now and again sharp showers of rain splattered down, soaking him. Once when he stopped to look down he recognised the cottage he lived in, tiny, belonging almost to another world. He could see the washing flapping in the orchard, hung between the orange trees; he could even see the old brown donkey grazing. Was his mother indoors? He suddenly felt very lonely up there on his own, with no one knowing where he was.

Hunger was getting the better of him. It really hurt.

He would have to go home soon, he just couldn't bear his emptiness much longer, but—oh! how could he go back without knowing what had happened to Federico?

Darkness fell swiftly over the hills that miserable October evening. One minute there was the rainy light and then, all of a sudden, it was dark. Fear clutched at Antonio. A long way off he could see the lights of the village, a thin line of bulbs which mapped the length of the main road and a scattering of lamps which shone from windows or lit up the lanes. But he couldn't see the houses, or anything else.

Everything seemed a long way off and the place he was in strange and sinister. He stumbled over boulders he could not see, going downwards now towards the village, afraid because there was no pathway and no moon to shine over the hillside for him.

Antonio had never realised how dark the night could be. He would have said that he wasn't afraid of the dark. A dark room holds no fear when you know the light switch is within reach. But now he was in the true dark and the only light was miles away, winking with the movement of the wind.

He swallowed the lump rising in his throat and yelled out, 'Federico!' as loudly as he could. His voice was caught by the surrounding hills and came back to him, 'Federico, . . . rico, . . . rico,' and it frightened him too much for him to call again.

For a time that seemed endless he went on and on, breaking into a run when he felt that the path was a straight one, but mostly sliding down the hill on his trouser seat, scratching his hands and face in the thorny branches that slapped unexpectedly into him, and scurrying like a frightened rabbit.

When he was beginning to lose all hope, when desperation was welling up inside him, ready to burst out in a torrent of useless tears, he saw a light. It wasn't far away although it was nowhere near the village. But it was real. In such darkness it was impossible to imagine that steadfast gleam.

He sniffed away the tears and struggled on, careless now of the tears and grazes and the rent in his trouser seam. Soon the outline of a house appeared, small,

stony like the hills that surrounded it and looking as though it had grown out of the barren ground. The light shone through the slats in the wooden shutters, illuminating a broken pathway across the few rows of potatoes and cabbages inside a walled garden.

A dog began to bark as Antonio climbed over the wall, too tired now to look for a gateway. A door opened and he was caught in its light, dwarfed by the shadow of the man who opened it.

'Who's there? What do you want?' his voice rang out abruptly. He was holding on to a big, rough-looking dog that wagged its tail and bared its teeth.

'I'm lost in the hills. I was trying to get back to the village when it got dark.'

'But you're only a boy! What are you doing up here? Are you alone?'

'Yes.'

'You'd better come in then. The dog won't hurt you.'

When he was close enough to see the man's face,

Antonio felt that he knew him. He was wrinkled and brown and his hair was a crinkled mixture of grey and white, just like the moustache.

'Do you want something to eat? I was just having my supper.'

Antonio looked about the room which was lit by the oil-lamp that had brought him here from the dark hill-side. It was like a barn for sheep or chickens, rough-walled, low-roofed, with a primitive chimney where a few logs smouldered and an earthenware cooking pot roasted in the heat.

The old man sent the dog back to his corner then reached for a blue-painted earthenware bowl on a shelf above the fireplace. He filled it from the pot over the fire with a soup of brown bread and cabbage leaves. Antonio, in his ravenous hunger, felt that even the fattest turkey wouldn't have tasted so good.

After watching him eat and listening to his story, told in snatches between the hurried mouthfuls, the old man said, 'You'd better come with me. I want to show you something.'

He picked up the oil-lamp and opened a roughly-made door at the far side of the room. There was the smell of animals and a rustling sound. Antonio followed him through the low doorway. A goat stared at him, its yellow eyes glowing in the lamplight. There was a big brown donkey, as patchy and bony-looking as its master, and in the far corner, half obscured by the darkness, another animal which didn't move.

The old man nudged Antonio. 'Have a look at him,' he said. 'It must be the donkey you're looking for.'

Hardly daring to believe, hardly daring to hope, Antonio went up to the beast lying alone. He went down on his knees and whispered, 'Federico,' and the donkey twitched his ears.

The man drew close with the lamp and Antonio could recognise his donkey then, thinner, rougher, with hair rubbed off in galls and sores, but it was none of this that roused his horror. He had never seen an animal mauled by dogs before; he could never have imagined that the teeth of two dogs could do such harm. He turned his head away, unwilling to look.

'Will he die?' he asked the man in a low voice.

'I don't know. He turned up early this morning, staggering, hardly able to keep on his legs, and I put him in here because I didn't know what else to do with him. I cleaned him up a bit, stopped the bleeding where it was bad, and gave him some hot bran with the hope of stirring him. Had to push it down his throat mostly.' He sighed and added, 'Looks like he wants to be left to die in peace.'

'No!' cried Antonio. 'I can save him. I know I can.'

'You might,' the old man conceded. 'He looks worse than he is. He hasn't lost too much blood. It's shock mostly. Those dogs must have well-nigh frightened him to death.'

Antonio bent again over the lank little donkey, still and lifeless almost in the bed of old bracken. He stroked his head and his nose. His hands smoothed all over the slashed and mud-splattered neck. He whispered the donkey's name time after time, pouring every ounce of love and care into the word. And he forgot all about the old man who watched him until he said, 'Well, if caring can get him on his legs again, you'll do it.'

Then he said, 'I remember you now, the pair of you. You were at the procession of San Anton. My Carbonero was eating the ribbons in his tail. Look at him over there! As old as I am and twice as artful. He knows there's something wrong.'

Antonio looked at him, struck by the note in his voice. 'You love your donkey, don't you? It's not wrong to love a donkey, is it? Everyone tells me I shouldn't love Federico.'

'I've only got Carbonero,' the other answered, by way of excuse or explanation, but he didn't answer the boy's question. He didn't need to.

The mascot

Antonio was left alone with the animals. The goat watched him with its yellow eyes and Carbonero's dark pupils were caught in the dull oily light. Federico was the only one that didn't look at him. His eyes were closed, covered by their long black lashes. But he listened. His ears twitched often as Antonio talked and talked to him, repeating phrases of love and encouragement. He didn't open his eyes and he didn't lift his head from the bracken, but the boy was sure that he recognised him.

It was raining again. Antonio fell asleep. In his utter exhaustion his sleep this time was dreamless and he was aware of nothing, not even the donkey's sweating body beneath him, until bright light burst into his eyes, accompanied by a noise and bustle entirely foreign to that silent stable.

Then Antonio did believe he was dreaming. Crowding into the close dark atmosphere and dispersing it by half a dozen bright torches dazzling here and there, were his father, Mestre Pedro, a couple of neighbours and two Civil Guards, the same who had called him to attention about the donkey long ago in the market place. All the men were soaked through and the guards had brought the dripping rain into the stable on their capes. They were all talking at once and the yellow-eyed goat bleated fractiously, adding to the confusion.

Antonio was yanked to his feet by his father and was startled by the fierce hug, instead of the admonishment he was expecting. 'I might have guessed we'd find you

with the donkey,' he said, and after that seemed lost for
words.

'What a boy!' one of the neighbours exclaimed. 'A
merry dance he's led us!'

'And all for an animal that does nothing but get him
into trouble.' This was from one of the guards. The other
was talking to the old man.

Señor Torres had found his voice again and with
hanging, sleep-dulled head, Antonio listened while his
father scolded him, telling him of the trouble he'd
caused, the hours they had all spent on the mountain
searching for him, the terrible state in which he had left
his mother.

'We expected to find you with a broken leg, if not a
broken neck. Have you nothing to say for yourself!' he

finished on an exasperated note, hardly able to be angry while he was still overwhelmed with relief.

'I wanted to find Federico. I knew he'd be hurt.'

'And now you've found him, what next?'

Antonio looked up at his father, his dark eyes eloquent. 'Please let me stay with him, just for tonight.'

Everyone fell silent, except Mestre Pedro, who let out an expression of contempt.

'Please,' he begged.

Mestre Pedro shone his torch over the donkey. He walked all round him, prodding him with his foot and his stick. Federico was motionless, seeming more dead than alive.

'The knacker's all he's fit for,' he pronounced at last. No one disagreed and he went on: 'He's not worth troubling about. I'll send the knacker up for him tomorrow. Little enough I'll get out of him, just the skin and the meat.' And he spat in disgust.

'You'd better come home,' said Antonio's father. 'Your mother's going crazy with worry.'

'Let me stay here, Papa. I'll come home by myself in the morning. I promise.'

'You can't do any good. You heard what Mestre Pedro just said.'

'I don't care. I don't want to leave him while he's sick.'

One of the Civil Guards shone his torch over Federico, catching Antonio's face in its beam. There was an intensity in his expression that the father couldn't ignore. He sighed and said, 'I don't know what your mother will say but . . . all right. Just for tonight. I want to see you home first thing in the morning, as soon as it's light.'

'It's three o'clock now,' remarked one of the neighbours. 'It'll be dawn within a couple of hours.'

They all went away, talking in loud grumbling voices. Antonio didn't listen to them. His world was the sick donkey, wanly visible in the gloomy light of the oil-lamp, safe until dawn. He couldn't sleep any more. Mestre Pedro's words had cut too deeply into his heart.

'You'll have to be on your feet tomorrow before the knacker arrives,' he desperately told Federico. 'If you're well again, he won't want to kill you.' And he sobbed over the donkey's back, his tears falling into the rough beige fur.

In the morning Federico lifted his head and could half sit up. He didn't attempt anything beyond this, only nuzzling at the bran Antonio held under his nose in his open palms and snuffling it all to the floor.

'You've got to go home now,' the old man reminded him. 'Those guards were very cross with me. They thought it was my fault that you were here. But I told them.'

Antonio couldn't eat the fried egg the old man offered him. He was too choked with despair.

'I can't go home,' he said, tears running down his cheeks again and falling into the plate. 'I can't leave Federico to face the knacker alone. How would you feel if it were Carbonero?'

The old man sighed. 'Stay if you want to. I've already told them. It's nothing to do with me.'

So Antonio stayed and the morning went by with agonising slowness. He didn't know what to say to

Federico any more. The donkey's sickness was of a kind that no medicines would cure. It was time he needed, time he hadn't got because Mestre Pedro refused to waste any more of it. But if he couldn't rouse himself from the apathy he had fallen into he would die anyway, without the help of the knacker.

Antonio pulled on his head and pushed at his rump. He used every kind of encouragement he could think of, even rage when there was nothing else left. But it was no good. Federico had decided that his legs wouldn't work. He stretched his neck out in the bracken again and completely ignored both Antonio and Carbonero who had come sniffing round.

In the early afternoon the two Civil Guards came toiling up the hillside. They looked very dour. They probably didn't like having their time wasted either.

'Why haven't you gone home?' they asked Antonio. 'You promised your father you'd be back by morning.'

Antonio bit his lip. He had no excuse to offer, at least none that would rouse their sympathy.

'Well?' the dark man demanded sharply. 'Have you forgotten?'

'I thought I'd just wait till the knacker came. I thought I might be able to get Federico on his feet before then.'

'What difference would it make?'

'Mestre Pedro might decide not to kill him.'

'He doesn't belong to Mestre Pedro any more. That's what we came to tell you. You weren't at home, so we had to come up here.'

Antonio looked at him, his unhappy face creased with puzzlement. 'Who does he belong to then?'

'He belongs to us, that is to say he belongs to the local command of the Civil Guard. We clubbed together to buy him. Thought we could do with a mascot.'

Antonio just stared, unable to believe a word.

'Of course,' put in the other, who was fair and blue-eyed, 'we shan't be able to keep him at the post. There's no room for a donkey. We hoped your father might let him graze in his orchard so that you could keep an eye on him when we're too busy ourselves.'

Antonio looked from one to another, hardly able to credit what they were saying. They must be joking, but, then, the Civil Guards were too serious to make jokes.

'Where is he?' said the dark one who had the southern accent like his father. 'We'd like to take another look at what we've bought.'

'He's still in the stable. He doesn't want to get better,' Antonio miserably confessed.

'Doesn't want to! We'll have something to say about that.'

The two guards entered the little stable and, after a brief consultation, went into action. Antonio didn't know how they managed it, although he was watching, but in less than a minute, and with a lot of noise, they had Federico on all fours, his tail twitching angrily, his head tossing.

'He's just stubborn. Now let's get him outside before he decides to sit down again.'

They dragged him out to the old man's garden and made him walk the length of it half a dozen times, laughing a great deal. It all seemed a big joke to them and there was nothing in the boy's tired face to suggest the turmoil that was going on inside him.

'Not much of a mascot,' the fair man turned to tell him. 'You'll have to get him into condition. We'll pay for the bran.'

'Do you really mean it?' Antonio asked. 'Did you really buy him from Mestre Pedro?' and then, 'But why?'

'Never mind why. You just get back home before you get into further trouble. The donkey can come back with us. He might need a bit of assistance.'

'Well, what are you waiting for?' the dark one demanded. 'Get on home.'

An immense grin took the shadows out of Antonio's grubby face. He hesitated a second longer, not knowing how to say thank you, not knowing whether thanks were even expected. He even felt like crying again.

Instead a shout of joy burst out of him as he turned and went running off down the track that would take him home, leaping and bounding with outflung arms; like a captive deer newly released in the forest. The two Civil Guards laughed as they watched him and Federico, between them, pricked his ears, wrinkled his nostrils and let out a long, high-pitched bray.